Both Sides of the Fence 4:

Bad Blood

Both Sides of the Fence 4:

Bad Blood

M.T. Pope

www.urbanbooks.net

Urban Books, LLC
97 N18th Street
Wyandanch, NY 11798

Both Sides of the Fence 4: Bad Blood

ISBN 13: 978-1-60162-423-9
ISBN 10: 1-60162-423-9

First Trade Paperback Printing September 2014
Printed in the United States of America

10 9 8 7 6 5 4 3 2 1

Distributed by Kensington Publishing Corp.
Submit Wholesale Orders to:
Kensington Publishing Corp.
C/O Penguin Group (USA) Inc.
Attention: Order Processing
405 Murray Hill Parkway
East Rutherford, NJ 07073-2316
Phone: 1-800-526-0275
Fax: 1-800-227-9604

More from M.T. Pope

Both Sides of the Fence 1
Both Sides of the Fence 2: Gate Wide Open
Both Sides of the Fence 3: Loose Ends
A Clean Up Man
May the Best Man Win

Novellas:

Lost Pages of Both Sides of the Fence Vol. 1
Stick Up Boys

Anthologies:

Anna J. Presents: Erotic Snap Shots Vol.1
M.T. Pope Presents: Boys Will Be Boys
Don't Ask, Don't Tell

Short Stories:

"Don't Drop the Soap"
"I Saw Daddy Doing Santa"

There is always someone looking for payback, always someone hunting for blood. Always!

—Ashley Black

Acknowledgments

This is my sixth full-length novel. I owe it all to God for blessing me with a wonderful gift that He chose to spring forth at the appointed time.

To my Mom, Lawanda Pope, a little woman with big strength. You make me smile every time I see you. You are the best mom in the world. I love you. My brothers and sisters: Shirley, William, Darnell, Darlene, Gaynell, Latricia, Nathon, and Yvette. I love you guys.

To my Pastor, Melvin T. Lee, and First Lady Tanya Lee, for coming out and showing love at my first book signing and everything else I do in this life. I promise Dad that the Christian fiction is still coming . . . lol. To all my Because He Lives church family members. I love you with only the love that God shines through me. WE ARE! . . . BECAUSE HE LIVES!

Carl Weber, once again, thank you for this opportunity, and all that you do. To the Urban Books home office family: Carl, Karen, Natalie, George (Gee), thank you.

To all the book clubs that hosted me, thank you for the love and support as well. Davida Baldwin, Oddball Designs (www.oddballdsgns.com): Thank you for another slamming cover.

I want to give a special thanks to couple of people who really supported me from a distance:

Martina Doss, thank you for giving me my first official review and selling my books down there in Atlanta. Also, thank you for calling me and letting me know how my books moved you. Thank you for hanging in there with me support-wise since book one. My literary friend, Karen Williams, who's a phone call away, thank you.

J'son M. Lee, man you are the best. We clicked from day one and we have so much in common. Thank you for answering the phone every time I call.

Dell Banks, for the encouraging phone calls and talks.

Anna J, for being one of the hardest working renaissance women in Philly. Leave something for somebody else to do . . . lol. To the people that encouraged me along the way. Kenneth Goffney, your words are so inspiring. I am glad to call you friend.

To my advance readers, Megan Lanier, Troy Lee, Darlene Washington, Nichelle Washington-Davis, thank you.

Deterrius Woods, an extraordinary Facebook buddy. Don't be afraid to finish your book. You have some great stories to tell, so get to work.

Kyeon, you have so much talent that it is ridiculous. So get started and get yourself out there.

To Yancey, keep going. Unstoppable hustle!

A Special shout out to Troy Lee for coming all the way from Philly just to get your books signed. I am still blown away by that. I will always remember that. Thanks for letting me borrow your name for the story, too.

My e-supporters and author friends: I may or may not have met you in person but you all are always encouraging and honest about my work: Megan Lanier, Iam Obsession, Allison Desse, Brandon Waters, Jahaziel Perez, Patrick Irené Plante, Aaron Brown, Shawna Brim, Troy Lee (Trent Muzak), Johnathan Royal, Ricardo 'Lore' Harrison, Gavin Fletcher, King Shamari Blake, Nicole Carter, Joy Ballard, Beverly Crowder, Orsayar Simmons, Yancey Uriah, LaDonna Smith, Michelle Dealwitit, King Brooks, Denzel Deshields, Shneka Kendrick, Robert White, Katia Denise, Deneshia Barnes, Malik Singleton,

Acknowledgments

Kenya Crockett, Tyeisha Downer, Nakenya Reeves, Sierra Kinchen, Tori R. Harrison, Della Dion, Koach Kabonna, Miz Jones, David Maurice Parker, Natalia Glover, Lenora Barksdale, Akima Rolle, Sabrina Gaddy, Reggie Marable, Jayne Brazelton, Chonda Bond, Linnette Brown, Nicki Williams,. Crystal Williams, Quanda Claud, Charnee Mccoy, De Ion Duncan, Mia Mikell Venable, Karen Bass, Andrew Rainey, Chris Covington, Amanda Lee, Lady Sasha, Trina Mcguire, Sabreen Clinton, Brandi Miller, Kevin Edwards, Adia Page, Rose Roses, Tamica Mindley, Jeana Anderson, Eder Rosa, James Maddox, Rahiem Brooks, Renita Johnson, Michelle Whelchel, Sandra Atueyi, Patrice Avery, Nikki Nik, James Whye Jr., Juanesia Faulks, Sonja Moore, Nakia Davis, Beth Sanders, Charmain Wilson, Chivonis Mills, Lil'mamabadd Smith, Tommy Pringle, Michell Ingram, Shaniyah Isallineed Shestruluv, Kim Woody-Slater, Jessica Goodman, LaTanya Baldwin, Joyce Duckett, Trifricia Lucas-Woodard, Tiawanna Anthony, Janice Gaston, Raven Simone Williams, Dianes Sykes, Melanie Tunstall, Monique Ford, Nikki Macnifcent, Jo'el Franklin, Debora Royal, Lakia Allen, Michelle Lawson, Rashawn Mayberry, Nicole Lewis, Schwana Haynes, Trey Crooks, Kiara Howard, and to the MANY that e-mail me and hit me up and spread the word. It is too many of you all to name. Know I appreciate all of you.

My old Walmart family: Shernae, Tamara, Renee, Gary, Ms. Val, Danuiella, Keisha, Wayne, Sharon. Thank you guys for your love and support. I still miss you guys . . . lol. But, not the work . . . lol.

If I left you out, put your name here:_____, because you are important to me too. *Smile*

I can be reached at www.facebook.com/authormtpope, www.twitter.com/mtpope, www.instagram.com/mtpope or e-mail me at chosen_97@yahoo.com. Thank you for the love.

Acknowledgments

PS: Please please leave book reviews on Web sites like Amazon, Barnes & Noble, and Books-A-Million. It means a great deal to authors no matter how you feel about the book.

Letter to the Reader

Hey everyone,

Are you surprised to see another installment of *Both Sides of the Fence?* I started this novel right after I finished book three and the juices/ideas weren't flowing at the time for the story so I decided that I would push it to the back burner and put out a non-sequel book or two before I attempted to give this one a go again. Well, after the success of *May the Best Man Win* and *A Clean Up Man,* I decided to go at this one again and the ideas came and started flowing together. So here you have it: *Both Sides of the Fence 4.*

I am so in love with the characters of this family and I am so happy to be writing about them once again. Drama follows these folks wherever they go. I love it. The characters have evolved in this book and you may or may not like them. Anyway, buckle up for some more drama.

Enjoy!

Prologue

Troy

Who Am I?

The past . . .

Blood was everywhere.
The piercing screams that I could still hear.
The revenge in his voice.
The pleading in hers.
The fear that filled my body as I stood there helpless and paralyzed.
What could I do?
I was a child.
What could I do?

A few months before the present . . .

I had surveyed them for some time now. The one I was watching now was named Ashley Black. She was a chocolate bombshell beauty, by the world's standards. But she was the enemy to me: she; her brother, Alex; and younger sister, Diana. They all had to be cut off at the root. I had to cut off this bad blood before they ruined anybody else's life, if they hadn't already. I was assigned to take them out of their misery. It was my destiny. What I was here for.

The scene was set, the props, all together for their final scene. I was the director and rewriter of their fate. They had been cast in their own downfall and I was glad to be the one to orchestrate it all.

I was sitting at a table in plain view of her. We were dining separately at a restaurant where you can eat outside. She was on her phone holding a lively conversation unaware of my presence or anyone's presence that is. She was laughing and smiling hard. That smile soon would fade. I would make sure of it personally.

She finally ended her phone call. It was time to make my move. I had to be bold. Level-headed. Calculated. I had to pull out all the stops and charm her into submission. Like I said before, I was groomed for this. This was my destiny.

I eased up from my table and casually walked over toward her table. "Excuse me, don't I know you?" I looked at her and smiled. "You're a model right?"

"Ahhh," she said and looked at me confused. "No, you must have me confused with someone else." She blushed, but she was trying to conceal it as she pushed her feathered hair out of her lowered face.

"No, I'm sure I've seen you on the cover of a magazine." I laid it on thick. I knew she wouldn't fall for this because it was such a weak line. It was my way of getting her attention and getting a feel for her, her present mental state. "You sure?"

"I think I would know about that." She spoke and then looked at me with an emotionless face.

I hoped I wasn't losing her. "Yes, you would." I nodded and then smiled again. "I'm sorry for the intrusion. I was sitting across the way and my mouth dropped because of your beauty." I didn't care who you were or how much attitude you had as a woman. You wanted to be called beautiful out in public or anywhere for that matter. Most women thrived on it. Some secretly. You could always tell who was getting it from home, a husband or a boyfriend. Or, none at all.

"I appreciated the compliment. Is there something else I could help you with?" She was polite and to the point. She was confident.

"Yes, I was wondering if it would be overstepping my bounds by asking to join you for a meal. I know this is weird and out of the blue, but I would like to get to know you better and since you haven't gone off on me yet, you could probably tolerate me for a few more moments of your time along with a meal."

"Are you serious?" she asked, confusion written all over her face.

I was anxious. Maybe I spoke too soon. Maybe I moved too soon. Was she about to give me the thrashing of my life with her tongue? I was kicking myself on the inside. I couldn't believe that I fucked this up. This was my only chance. She was the one I needed to start with. How could I be so arrogant?

"What kind of girl do you take me for?" she asked and put one of her hands on her chest.

There was an awkward moment of silence. What could be said to clean up this mess that I made? I was at her mercy.

Then she giggled. "I'm joking, have a seat. I'll give you a chance. What's the worst that could happen? Besides, I didn't want you to plague another woman with that tired line of rap you used on me."

I instantly exhaled. I didn't even know I was holding my breath. I hoped she couldn't tell. I pulled out the chair and sat down across from her. I didn't say anything at first.

"I'm sorry about the weak line I used. I am new at this and I didn't really know how to approach you," I lied.

"Well, that's nice to hear. I am new on the dating scene as well. I guess we will be each other's fresh start." She smiled. She had his smile.

I was excited. I got in. I was successful.

"So, Ash . . . I mean what can I call this beautiful lady sitting in front of me?" I was hoping that she didn't catch that slip-up. I wanted to curse my own self out for that one.

"For a minute I thought that you were calling me by my name." She laughed.

"No, I was saying that I was so *ash*amed that I didn't come over earlier." I laughed with nervousness in my voice.

"Oh, I think your timing was impeccable."

"Oh, really." I looked at her with curiosity. "How so?"

"Well, truthfully I was spying you out as well."

"Really?" I was genuinely smiling now.

"Yes, you are quite a handsome guy yourself. I saw how the waitress was eyeing you down and a few of the other ladies. Who wouldn't want to get to know you? And to answer your question, my name is Ashley."

"Wow, I am truly amazed. Here I was thinking I was tracking you, but you had me in eyesight all along."

"What is this truly amazed man's name?" she asked me.

"Troy. My name is Troy."

"What a nice name, Troy. It is nice to meet you, Troy." She reached across the table to shake my hand.

I followed suit. There was a spark as soon as our hands united.

"Oow." She pulled back and then laughed. "Sparks. I guess this is meant to be."

"Yes, I believe in fate. You know, destiny."

"This destiny chick is going to have to wait, because I got you now. She missed out."

We both laughed. She didn't know that destiny had won. Their fates were sealed.

Chapter 1

Ashley

Forever My Lady

"'I always feel like somebody's watching me,'" I sang along to the classic Rockwell song that played on my satellite radio in my car. I loved classic music or music that withstood the sands of time. My grandmother always said I had an old soul. I felt like it sometimes too.

Have you ever had the feeling that you were being followed, but couldn't put your finger on it? Maybe I was feeling paranoid or maybe it was the song that brought back memories all of the drama from these last few years. Some of it still had me on edge at times. I had only been back in Baltimore a year and a half after living in California for a few years and now I was fresh into my first weeks at my new job. When I finished my degrees in human services, I applied and was offered a position at a nonprofit organization for dysfunctional families called Inside-Out: A Family Inside and Out. I wanted to channel what I learned from my family to help others. Our family had been through so much and survived that it was the only logical career choice to make.

California and Baltimore were like night and day when it came to living. Like New Yorkers, Californians moved fast and almost never slept. Here in Maryland things shut down early. I liked California, but Maryland was home for me. I had expectations of slowing it down and taking life easy when I touched down in Baltimore. I reconnected with one of my girls from high school, Jasmine, and now we were kicking it on the regular. She was still cool people to me even though she could be weird at times. I didn't have many girls as friends, for drama purposes, but now I was looking for a calmer lifestyle and friends. So she was one of the only ones I paid any attention to in high school. I was a hothead not too long ago, but all that ever got me was in trouble. So here I was living the good life as a full-fledged adult. It is crazy to have to pay your bills and manage your money but I had good training from my parents and I was adjusting.

I was now living on my own and with a new career and even a budding relationship with my first boyfriend. Troy was such a nice guy and so attentive. He was so new and refreshing. I could admit that it was scary as well. We had been dating for some months and it was going strong. He made me smile every time I thought about him. He never pushed me to go all the way and I was glad that he was so patient.

I pulled into the local Dunkin' Donuts about a mile from my job. I had to get my coffee and doughnut fix before I made my way into the office. I opened the door to my midsized SUV and stepped out one leg at a time. My four-inch heels looked good on the end of my statuesque legs. I had on a tan, one-piece, knee-length dress that was appropriate for the office environment and I still turned heads out in public. I loved being a lady.

I took nice small strides as I walked to the door. My real hair, which flowed and ended right past my shoulders, was tousled slightly by a gust of wind into my face. I removed it as I made it to the door of the establishment. A nice gentleman smiled and opened the door for me.

"Thank you," I spoke and then smiled back at him. Life was good for me. I walked toward the counter and stood in line with my order on my mind.

"Welcome to Dunkin' Donuts, what can I get for you today?" the polite, older, Hispanic-looking woman said as she smiled at me.

"I'll take a medium French vanilla iced coffee, a plain bagel, and cream cheese. I would also like two Old Fashioned Donuts."

"I see you still like old things," someone almost hissed from behind me. They were close up on me and it made me tense up a little. My heart dropped because I knew the voice all too well.

"Oh, ah, hey, Antoinette," I turned and spoke to my ex-lover with nervousness in my voice. She was still as tall as my father and thick, too. She looked manlier than I remembered her.

"Ashley, you are growing up so nicely. And you still stacked like a brick house I see." She looked me up and down with what I knew were impure thoughts running through her mind. She still looked the same with the exception of a few gray hairs sprinkled in her hair.

"Thank you." I smiled politely. I secretly cringed on the inside from looking at my choice clearly for the first time. I didn't know what in the hell I was thinking when I was with her. She was old enough to be my mother and she wasn't all that attractive. They said I was rebellious, but I knew for sure I was desperate as well. Yes, desperate summed it up for me.

"Ma'am, your order is ready." The cashier interrupted us. I silently thanked God for the escape.

"Well, nice seeing you, Antoinette, but I have to be going." I grabbed my food and made a quick exit to the entrance of the store. The sounds of my heels could be heard on the floor because I was pressed to get out of there and to avoid any type of scene.

"Wait up, Ash; let me holler at you for a minute."

Holler? I wondered why she was speaking slang at her age. She sounded like my father trying to play like he was one of us, but was so out of tune with today's slang.

I kept going and stopped when I got outside the store. I was already embarrassed as it was. Being in her presence made me uncomfortable, being that our past history was such a crazy one I didn't want to be around her for a long time. She had a crazy streak and I didn't want to do or say anything to trigger it today.

"So what have you been up to lately?" she asked, while looking me directly in my eyes. She continued, "Word around the way was that you were all the way in California living the Hollywood life. I know you did a couple of bitches while you were up there. You lay that tongue on them or what?"

Damn, I know people aren't sitting around talking about me. Her ass must have been tracking me or something. Technology is something. Her ass could have been one of them fake Facebook or Twitter followers. The hell if I knew.

"Nothing, I'm living my life," I spoke, bypassing all of that other nonsense she spat out of her mouth. I tried to hold my nerves on the inside but my eye started to twitch a little. I wanted to get away from her.

"That's good. Are you seeing anybody?"

"Now that's not any of your business," I spoke with a shot of adrenaline and confidence that came from out of nowhere.

"Wow, you still a feisty and spicy sister I see." She laughed a little.

The nervousness in me subsided a little. Maybe she had mellowed out too. "Yeah, that's me, through and through," I said and then smiled. I had calmed down quite a bit since my teenage years, but I knew that I still had a few sparks of wildness left in me. "Look it's been nice but I actually have to run." I lied about the nice part, but what she didn't know wouldn't hurt her.

"Yeah, okay."

I heard her speak as I walked away and toward my car. I surely didn't want her to see what car I drove because I didn't want her to know anything about me even though we'd been sexually intimate. I hurried and hopped into my car as fast as I could. I wanted to pull off and be ghost in a matter of seconds, but I wasn't fast enough because she was beside my car before I could pull off.

"I still love you, girl. I know I messed up but I want another chance to make it right." She looked serious. "Plus you're old enough now. I want to stamp my name on that pussy of yours with my tongue again."

"Antoinette, that is not going to happen. What we had is gone and it was wrong."

"Did you hear me when I said that I still love you, girl?" she asked, skipping right past what I had spoken a second earlier.

She was leaning on the frame of my driver's side car door looking at me hard. I squirmed in my seat a little. Her focus on me made me feel really uncomfortable. I watched her close her eyes and then she waved her nose in the air like she smelled some fresh bread being baked.

"Damn, girl, I can still smell your pussy. You still fresh like a bouquet of roses. Girl, let me get another taste of that goodness. There's a motel right down the block that I can take you to and flip you over and—"

"Anyway." I squeezed my legs closed and aggressively interrupted her trip down memory lane. "I heard you and I know you heard what I said. That . . . is not . . . going to happen. It's over. Read the eulogy and then bury the coffin, sugar." I put my car in reverse and pulled off before she could get another word in. She fell and hit the ground because she didn't think I would pull off like I did. I was not in the mood to go back and forth with her or anybody for that matter.

"Bitch, it's not over until I say it's over," she yelled as I pulled off. "You'll always be mine! Always!"

I shook my head in shame as I drove down the street. "I can't even go to Dunkin' Donuts in peace." I said as I looked over to my food, which was in the passenger seat. I checked my rearview mirror a few times to see if she was following me in her car. I exhaled when I realized that she was not behind me. At least I hoped she wasn't following me, since I didn't know what she was driving or if she was driving. Here I was trying to be the new and improved Ashley and people from my past wanted to drag me back down. They didn't want me to dig back down and bring back ol' girl, because it wouldn't be pretty.

I walked into work with a smile on my face even though I was agitated on the inside. *How could she embarrass me like that in public? Did my no really warrant that type of response? Calm down, Ashley, calm down.*

In my field of work I saw families who were in crisis situations and trying to work things out. I had two families I was working with for a few weeks who were on the verge of killing one another; one family was from the deep part of the hood and the other one was from a Baltimore County area. The one from the Baltimore County area was much like my family. They both had serious issues and were recommended to us by the State of Maryland for rehabilitation. I was excited and apprehensive at the same time when it came to helping these families. I didn't want to do anything that would promote further damage.

I walked into my office and turned on my computer. I had a video message that popped up as soon as I logged on. It was from Troy. I instantly perked up and a smile spread across my face. I listened to the brief message of him asking to go out to get something to eat. I immediately dialed his number on the PC and hoped he was available to talk. When his face popped up I knew that he was available. We talked for a few minutes and scheduled a date for after work.

Troy was a gentleman. He was the best thing that happened to me in a long time. He was a very "strapping" guy, as my father said it.

He was a tall guy, but very mild mannered and patient. He was handsome and very easy on the eyes. I was really excited to be with him. He was a few years younger than me, but he looked mature for his age. He was a detective and a good one, too. Only problem was that I didn't tell him about my past. You know, the lesbian thing.

My mom and dad asked if I had the conversation with him and I lied and told them that I had a very open and honest conversation with him. Yes, I know what you are saying. I should have known better by now. I did, but this was a new situation for me. This was my first relationship with a male. I had to feel him out first and see if he was ready for that type of information. That may sound like an excuse but I was scared. Yes, I said scared. I am scared of being rejected. Plus, how do you tell a guy that you were once a carpet muncher? I asked God for forgiveness as soon as I left their house.

I hated that I couldn't be honest with Troy, but he was homophobic to the max. I had seen him literally cringe in the presence of someone in "the life." It was like he was terrified of them. He would tense up and clam up tightly. I didn't know how I was going to do it but I really needed to let him know so I could get my mind cleared. I decided that tonight would be the night that I would tell him.

"Yes, tonight will be the night." I nodded my head and adjusted myself in my chair, getting ready to start my day at work.

Chapter 2

Alex

Party Over Here

Being a sports agent had it perks. Right now I was in the club with a few ladies clamoring for my attention. The music was pumping loudly and there were women everywhere. It was an invite from a professional football player for Baltimore who shall remain nameless. There were bottles popping all over the place. This was a party of all parties. Being that I was never really a party person; at first it was a culture shock for me. Even with all the drama that my family had been through I had never been in a wild environment like this one. Scantily dressed ladies were everywhere and some even confused me for a professional player because I was built well. I was enjoying myself too much to tell them that I was a sports agent. It felt good to get out of my shell after all of this time. Who knew that there was a party animal that lived inside of me and was ready to go crazy, like I was doing right at this moment?

"So you going to let me take you home tonight?" I whispered into the ear of this chick who was thick in all the right places and had her breasts up against me like she want me to suck on them right then and there. Yes, I was still freaky but I didn't get down like that in public; maybe in a bathroom stall or something but not out in the open.

I wasn't sideshow material. I did all my nasty shit behind closed doors. The whole time I was checking her neck out to see if she had an Adam's apple like me. If you knew my past you'd know why I did this. If her hands were as big as mine were then I made up an excuse and moved on to the next lady of interest. Shit was real out here. Nobody was who or what they said they were. I had been some places and seen some things that I shouldn't have been exposed to at an early age as I was. But as the saying goes, "What doesn't kill you will make you stronger." My ass should be as strong as the Incredible Hulk or something for all of the stuff I been through and made it out of.

Living on my own now had its advantages and banging girls' backs out in the comfort of my own apartment was one of them. Now I didn't sleep with as many women as the jocks I worked for, but I got my fair share and they weren't bottom feeders either. Well, maybe a few.

"Hey, Lex, are you trying to go to the after party at my crib? I'm ready to blow this place and take this thing all the way live," the athlete I was invited here by asked me.

I wasn't about to turn down some free liquor and a couple of groupies trying to get into the pants of anybody close to or assumed to be close to the professional athlete. He was semi well-known and he sure partied like a rock star. I was all game.

"Hell yeah." I hopped off of the sofa in one of the VIP rooms we were partying in and was ready to go get white boy wasted.

A few more folks got up and we all made our way to our cars and followed my client to his house. We pulled up to a gated community about twenty minutes from the club that we left. It was close to one in the morning. I knew I had to go to work in the morning, but the party animal in me told the responsible me to chill the fuck out.

This guy was making good money because he was living up in a double-story condominium with all of the bells and whistles to go with it: Jacuzzi, swimming pool, and exercise room. It was about twenty to thirty people who filed into his residence and it didn't take long before the party got pumped up again. Man, I was drinking like a fish in water. I knew I was going to be paying for it in a few hours but I still didn't care. I was making up for all of the years of being the "good" twin. I was now the "party over here" twin. I was partying every weekend.

I woke up to a dog licking my face. I opened my eyes slowly because I felt fucked up all over. I was in a bed with my shirt off and a bottle of vodka next to me.

"Ahhh," I softly moaned as I tried to sit up. It was a slow process but I finally got up on the side of the bed. As I put my foot down, I felt something mushy and prayed to God that it wasn't what I thought it was. I peered over a little bit to see.

"Shit," I groaned and shook my pounding head and then I pulled my foot out of the pile of puke. I looked around the room to see if there was something I could wipe it off with. There was nothing, but I did notice a chick lying half naked on the floor.

"Damn, did I fuck her?" I wondered out loud. She was naked from the waist up so I knew I at least sucked on her breast. I was a breast man for sure. My pants were still intact so I assumed that I didn't. I didn't even know who this chick was. All I remember was having a few drinks with her and talking about frogs or some shit. I had learned that men would listen to anything from a chick to get laid.

I had no clue as what happened last night. I looked at my watch and it read seven-thirty. I had an hour to get home and then to work. Even though I got drunk, I still made it to work on time even if I had a hangover from hell. The sudden urge to piss hit me and I slowly rose to my feet and went on a journey to relieve my bladder.

Man, there was limp bodies everywhere. The music was still on blaring. I was surprised that the neighbors didn't call the police, but, hey, when you have money I guess you don't have to really worry about authority like the rest of the world.

"That was one hell of a party." I smiled as I stepped over a victim on the floor in front of the door of the room I woke up in. He was contorted with one of his arms behind his back as he laid on it. It looked painful. "His ass is going to feel that for a few days."

Since this was the first time I was in this dude's house, I had no clue as to where the bathroom was located. He had a lot of rooms in this condo. It made me wonder what he was paying for this place.

When I located the bathroom I was relieved. I went in, relieved myself, washed my hands, and made my way downstairs. Most of the house was still asleep so I walked around as quiet as I could trying to get out as fast as I could.

"My movies!" I exclaimed. I covered my mouth to hush my pitch. I was at his front door getting ready to leave when I remembered that I let him hold some of my DVDs and Blu-rays a few days ago. I needed to get those back. From the look of his house he was not the most organized person. I like to keep my movies and things pristine. Especially since almost everything was digital now. I was collector of movies and music and I rarely let people hold my things. I doubled back and located his entertainment room.

"Wow, dude is a slob." I shook my head. *I guess money can't buy you cleanliness, but he damn sure has enough to pay someone to clean up this mess. I hope they are on vacation or something.*

"He doesn't ever have to worry about me giving him any more of my things ever again," I grumbled as I located a pile of DVDs and Blu-rays that was piled up without any protection on them. I cringed. I was so pissed that I grabbed the stack of about ten and walked out of his house. I would call him later to get the cases that went with them.

I got home, laid the discs on my coffee table, and quickly prepared myself for work. I was out of my house in record time. I made it to work with a little time to spare. I had a slight hangover and vowed again that I wouldn't drink at a party so hard the next time I went out, but I knew that would be like talking to the wall that I just parked my car in front of.

I got off of the elevator and walked into the office area where I worked with a couple of other sports agents and made my way pass the receptionist desk that was made of a circle with offices spread around it. There was a new girl sitting at the desk. For some reason this company couldn't keep a receptionist too long. She was beautiful and ripe for the picking. I instantly perked up and put a devilishly handsome smile on my face like only I could do. I had a very brief movie of me fucking her over the side of my desk or something like that before I got up to the desk.

"You must be new here, because the sun seemed to be shining a little bit brighter outside. You are like a bright ray of sunshine." I looked directly into her eyes as I spoke.

"Who are you and why are you at my desk?" she spat out. There wasn't an inkling of a smile on her face. She was going to be a hard nut to get I could see.

"I'm sure you've heard of me. I'm Alex Black. I'm an agent here. You didn't see my name on the door to my office?"

"You are one of many. How can I help you today?" she asked brushing past what I said.

Damn, this girl going hard. Her pussy must be fortified like Fort Knox. I was going to get the combination to the pussy if it was the last thing I did. Mind you this was a white chick with this blunt attitude. They are usually a bit more reserved in the work environment from my past experiences. But I guessed that was a thing of the past nowadays. Everyone was wild.

"Don't worry you'll get to know me very shortly. Believe me," I said; then I turned and walked toward my office.

"Yeah, okay, keep on believing that," I heard her say, doubtfully, as I walked away.

I peeked back over my shoulder and gave her one last look and a wink. She sucked her teeth and continued to do whatever she was doing before I walked up to her desk and apparently into her space. I liked a strong woman because they fucked harder and sucked harder, like they had a point to prove.

I walked into my office and flopped down in my highly comfortable chair. I was exhausted. Most of the time, my hangovers consisted of exhaustion. I was testing the girl out front. I didn't really want her per se. Well, if the opportunity came along I sure would knock her off but right now I was too tired to do anything. All I wanted to do was go home and sit in front of the television and chill out by myself. But I was at work and I had to do some work. I loved my paycheck and the things that it afforded me.

I turned on my PC and looked at my schedule for the day. I only had two clients today and I was relieved that it was only minor issues. *I might check and see if my boss will let me leave early.* It wasn't long before my next client came in and I began my workday. All I was thinking about the whole time was making it to the end of the day or my day that is.

Chapter 3

Jasmine

Mrs. Alex Black

"Mrs. Jasmine Black. Mrs. Alex Black," I repeated my new name as I twirled around and around in my wedding dress in front of a mirror in my bedroom. I loved the way I looked in my wedding dress. I was beautiful and radiant.

"We are going to have a beautiful life together, Alex. You wait and see." I kissed him on the cheek. I had a life-sized cutout of him in a tux that I ordered from off of the Internet. I couldn't wait until that day came when I walked down the aisle and became his wife. We were going to have the perfect life together: me, him, our three kids, and possibly a dog and cat. Sarah, Jeremiah, and Timothy; I had all of our children's names picked out. I bought their clothes already for the first year of their lives. I had their bedroom sets in storage and I even had some stuff for the house we were going to have together. I had it all worked out. I was waiting for Alex to pop the question. I had a feeling it was going to be very soon.

I put on my music as I got dressed for work. I put on my scrubs and as I continued to plan my life with Alex.

"Momma, it is almost about that time." I spoke as I picked up the picture of my deceased mother from off of my dresser. She was so pretty in the wedding dress she had on. Now it was going to be my turn to walk down the aisle in it and I looked as good as she did in it, too.

"Hussy, you'll never be as good as me." I heard my mother's voice and then looked around the room.

"Is that you, Momma?" I quivered a little as I looked at her picture and then around the room.

"Look at you. You're ugly." I heard her voice again. This time it was louder. I turned and looked behind me. No one was there. I dropped her picture and watched it hit the carpeted floor.

"Momma, I'm trying. I'm trying to be like you. I want to be pretty like you," I said as I stared at her picture.

"You are never going to get a man with that ugly body you have. I should have aborted you if I knew you would have ended up like this. Worthless."

"That's not true, Momma; that's not true. I'm beautiful. Daddy said so," I yelled and then grabbed the sides of my head shaking it from side to side trying to bore her voice from out of my mind. I couldn't because she was every-where I went: in my dreams, at work, and even in the car. She was dead yet still nagging me from beyond the grave. My daddy had died of a heart attack at an early age. I was about eight years old, but I remember him coming into my room every day to wake me.

"Hey, princess." He would pull the covers off of me and to the bottom of the bed. I would smile and then stretch my arms wide out to the side and then in front of me and wait for Daddy to give me a hug.

"Hey, Daddy," I greeted him back. We embraced for a few seconds and then he would pull away.

"You ready to let the world see your smile?" He asked me this every morning. It made me feel so special, like I was the prettiest girl in the world. "Mommy is getting your lunch ready so we have to hurry up and get downstairs for breakfast. You don't want to make her mad do you?" He looked at me with loving yet concerned eyes. My daddy was a great guy. He was so nice and

mannerly. I never heard him say a harsh word or even raise his voice. My mother was a different story. She was hell on wheels.

"No, Daddy," I said as I would hurry toward the bath-room to wash up and get dressed. I would hurry down the stairs, eat my breakfast, and then Daddy would walk me to the bus stop to wait for the bus.

"Then you died, Daddy, and left me with this witch of a mother," I said as I picked up his picture and squeezed against my chest with my arms. I pulled it away and looked at it again. He was a full-figured guy but I didn't see that as a child. He was Daddy to me. My mother would call him "tubby" and "lard butt" all the time, but he would smile at her and go into the living room to watch television. He was such a gentleman.

My mother was a great cook. I thought it was her cooking of all of the fried foods that killed my daddy. My daddy would still be here if it weren't for her constantly feeding him all those greasy meals. My nice, handsome father always treated me like a lady. Alex reminded me a lot of my father. Alex had all of the qualities that my daddy had but he was fit and healthy.

"But I'm all right now, Daddy. Cancer took her away from here about three years ago, as you already know, and she went kicking and screaming. I know she's not with you in heaven, Daddy. But she gone from here and I'm glad. I need to get me a man like you and get her nagging voice in my head to go away.

"I'm going to be Mrs. Alex Black soon, Dad, and then I will be better to him then she was too you. I promise." I had to figure out how.

No one knew that was my life as a child and teenager, because I hid it well. Momma did as well. Anytime we had visitors she was a totally different person. She was so nice at times that I wanted to scream out, "Who are you and

where the fuck did you send my mother?" But, most of
the time I sat still and smiled like I was trained to do. My
mother was "a child should be seen and not heard unless
I'm whipping that ass" kind of parent. My daddy tried but
he wasn't any match for my momma.

Sometimes I wanted to ask him what made her be the
way she was, but I kept it all on the inside. I strived and
excelled in school so I could make a better life for me and to
get away from her. I succeeded and now I was a private
duty nurse. I loved taking care of people for a living and
it brought me great joy to help people get better. But it
didn't distract me from the loneliness that I felt when I
got home and closed my door. I felt rejected and like an
outcast. If it weren't for my only friend, Ashley, I thought
I would have gone crazy by now.

"Let me get myself together," I said as I looked in the
mirror on my bedroom dresser. I was a chocolate girl.
Good cheekbone structure and full lips. I was a little
pudgy in the right and wrong places. My shoulder-length,
pin-curled hair was all mine. I smiled a weak smile and
then walked across my plushy carpeted room and exited
my bedroom.

I got all that I needed for the day and exited my apartment. I stopped right in front of my door, turned around,
and looked ahead. A smile crept across my face. It was
a smile filled with hope. Alex lived right across the hall
from me. How, you say? After Ashley and I reconnected
when she came back from California, she mentioned that
she had found her own apartment, but Alex had a little
trouble finding what he wanted. I mentioned to her that
the apartment across from me was vacant and I would
see if the rental office would let him look at it to see if he
liked it.

I had to let the lesbian clerk suck on my pussy a few
times to get her to hold it for me. I would do anything for

my husband-to-be. Now I'm not going to lie, she had my ass almost crawling up the walls backward on my hands and feet like I was that possessed chick in that *Exorcist* movie. I was in need of a good nut anyway.

"See you when I get home, baby." I kissed his door.

I turned around to see one of my elderly neighbors looking at me like I had lost my mind.

"Good morning, Mr. Coleman," I greeted him. He looked at me, shook his head, and then put his finger on his finger reader to get into his apartment.

As I walked by him I could have sworn I heard him call me a "crazy bitch," but I kept on walking because I could have been mistaken.

Chapter 4

Troy

Let's Get Intimate

Beautiful. This was what I thought as I sat in the restaurant and watched Ashley walk over to the table where I was seated. She had confidence and energy in her stride across the room. She seemed like she had life by the antlers and was commanding every move in her life. She had tiny moments of shyness since I'd met her, but that was starting to dissipate over time. We were out in a sophisticated part of Columbia, Maryland. It was a nice restaurant off of the beaten path. It was a high-maintenance establishment and you had to have connections to get in, which I did. I rose from my chair as she approached the table.

"Hello, honey." She greeted me with a nice tight hug. The way her breasts felt up against my body as she hugged me sent me into overdrive. I had my arms wrapped around her waist that was a beginning to a nice, round behind. She was fabulous. I pulled back and pulled out her chair for her. She was well bred and respectable. She sat down and I scooted her chair up so she could be closer to the table. I sat on the opposite side and stared at her for a few seconds.

"What's wrong? Is there something on my face?" She quickly picked up her purse and found a mirror before I could stop her.

"No, no, Ashley." I shook my head as I reached my hand over to pull the mirror down that she had held to her face. "You are simply beautiful. You're a beautiful work of art and a spitting image of your heritage."

"Thank you," she said, blushing.

"How was your day?" I asked.

"My day was quite wonderful." She smiled. "And it's even better now that I am here with you." She reached her hand over and put it on top of mine that was resting on the table.

"Same here," I added. "I can't believe I found you. You are so what I was looking for."

"I was what you've been looking for?" she asked. "Is that a line you've used on past girlfriends?"

"No, I mean it. I looked for you. I mean I knew that I would find you. You have all that I need to complete my life."

"That's really flattering." Her teeth showed as she smiled even harder now.

"No, it's the truth. You will see." I spoke wholeheartedly.

"Yes, we shall see. So what makes me so special?" She posed a very valid question.

"Have you looked in the mirror lately? You are the whole package. What man wouldn't want you?"

"That is nice to hear."

"It's even nicer to say. You are my destiny." I reached over the table and put my hands over hers and looked at her attentively as I spoke.

"Okay, okay, enough about me. What about you? I want to know more about you," she asked as she looked at me as intently as I did her moments ago.

"More about me?" I asked. I was a private person and I really didn't share my personal information with anyone but I was comfortable with her now so I guessed it would be all right to share some of me with her.

"Yes, is there an echo in the room?" She laughed lightly. "Okay, what do you want to know?"

"You said on one of our first dates that you didn't like talking about family, but I am curious to know. But, if it is too painful I'll give you a pass."

"You are right, I don't like talking about it as I stated early on, but I am close enough to you and your family to let you know about my family now. Are you ready?" I breathed in and exhaled as to compose myself for what I was about to say.

"Yes, whenever you're ready." She spoke seriously and with attentiveness, as if I was one of her clients.

"I was born and raised in the slums of Baltimore City. Both of my parents were killed in a drug deal gone wrong. They were killed execution style right in front of me." A tear escaped my eye as I recalled the moment in those few seconds. It was all so real all over again. The blood, the screams of my mother before they shot my father, and then the silence of the room as they killed her and left me in the room with blood that covered the kitchen floor and walls.

"I was only eight at the time, but I was strong. I didn't cry or scream. I left the house and walked outside and sat on the front steps. In the neighborhood that I lived in most people didn't care and they didn't ask questions so I sat on the steps in bloody pajamas in broad daylight for close to an hour before someone even came to check on me. You see my parents had scammed and tricked so much in the neighborhood that people didn't bother me or even let their children play with me. They weren't better; they were more decent lowlifes than my parents were, if that makes any sense."

"Oh my goodness, I didn't know. That's horrible." She shook her head in disbelief. One after another, tears rolled down her face.

"Yes, it was." I lowered my head trying not to let on that the story was getting to me as well. "I was passed around from family member to family member because no one wanted the 'drug addict's' baby. I swore from then on that I would make something of myself and never look back. And I never have."

"I'm so sorry that you had to go through all of that." She reached her hand across the table and wiped the tears that were falling from my eyes.

"It's all right. Enough about me; I want to know more about you. You haven't been as forthcoming either."

"Okay, what do you want to know?" she asked and then smiled. The wrinkles in her forehead showed her nervousness.

Chapter 5

Ashley

The Main Course

"Tell me one thing about you that most people don't know about you," Troy asked and then looked at me intently, waiting for me to answer.

I shifted in my chair. I crossed my legs. I cleared my throat. All of it was a stall so I could come up with something to say. I had no clue as to where to start. I was young but had so much going on the last past couple of years that most people didn't know about me.

"One thing . . . about me . . . that most people don't know?" I pondered and stalled, again, all at the same time.

"Yes, that was the question." He smiled and then the dimples in his face cheeks appeared. It made me feel at ease. His eyes were so warm and inviting. "Is that too much to ask?"

"No, no, no, it's not that heavy." I was still searching my mind for something that wasn't too crazy or wild to tell him.

"Are you sure now?" he asked.

"I'm sure. Give me a minute."

"You have all the time in the world," he said and then chuckled some. Pretty soon he started to hum the theme song to the old game show named *Jeopardy!*

"I have two fathers." I blurted it out.

Silence.

Silence.

The look on his face was blank.

My stomach started to churn. What was he about to do? Explode in a tirade? Flip the table over and walk off?

"Okay," he said in an even tone, as if what I said didn't matter to him.

"So all you're going to say is 'okay'?" I said with more emotion than necessary. I didn't think he'd be so calm. It made me calm.

"Yes, what do you want me to say?" He smiled again and then folded his hands together on the table.

"So you don't have any questions?" I asked and then I look at him and waited.

"Wellllll, since you are waiting so patiently let me ask you a question." He paused, adjusted his tie and then spoke, "How is that possible?"

"I found out awhile back that my dad, the man you know as Mr. Black, is not my biological father. My mother had an affair with a man who is now deceased."

"Amazing." He shook his head in awe. "So you never got to meet this man."

"Briefly during an outing with my mother when I was young but he died before we ever got the chance to get to talk or get to know one another." I spoke solemnly.

"Do you know anything about him?"

"Well, his name is James Parks and he was a 'pretty wild but passionate guy,' from what my mother tells me." I shrugged my shoulders after I finished talking. I then took a sip of the complimentary glass of water that was sitting near my plate setting.

"I take it he's not a topic of discussion in your family?" Troy asked with curiosity written all over his face.

"No, he's not. We pretty much stay away from that topic of discussion. No need in opening closed or old wounds."

"Yes, old wounds can be quite dangerous," he said and then looked off for a moment and then he looked back at me. "So were you ever mad at your mother for such a betrayal? Did you feel like she owed you an explanation?"

"That situation was between her, James Parks, and my father. I'm a product of an unfortunate yet fruitful situation."

"That is true." He nodded his head. "Did your father ever retaliate or step out on your mother?"

"Wow." I shook my head in shock. "Did you really just ask me that?"

"I am so sorry. That was the inquisitiveness in me asking those questions. I am deeply sorry."

"No, I'm a big girl. I can handle myself well. I was caught off guard by the question. But to answer your question, he's not that type of man." Truth was he did sleep with James Parks but I didn't think it was on a retaliation basis, but Troy did not need to know all of that. That would be too much for him to handle. Truth was, I still had a hard time thinking about it as well.

"No, he doesn't seem like the type," he agreed. "So do you think about him at all? Think about what it would be like to have talk to him while he was alive?"

"Not really," I answered. "He's dead."

"Why so cold?" Troy asked.

"I'm not cold. That is the truth. Besides, my father did an excellent job of being a father to me." I spoke confidently.

"So if you had one wish, it wouldn't be to have one conversation with him or a hug?"

"No." I shrugged my shoulders. "I'm sure he was a great guy. In fact, I know that he was a great guy. That is why I don't wish to dig up buried things." Memories of sitting in my grandmother's living room in California and going through photo albums and some home movies flooded my mind. I was satisfied with having those memories.

"Well, if that is how you feel." He looked away from me for a moment, like he was looking out into space. It kind of freaked me out a bit.

"Are you okay?" I asked in concern for Troy. He looked a little peaked in the face.

"Yes. Yes, I am fine." He was smiling again. "Let's order some food and enjoy this lovely evening together."

Chapter 6

Alex

Pop-ups

When I got home from work today all I wanted to do was strip down, shower, eat, and watch a movie on the sofa in front of my big-screen plasma television. It was an earned comfort. I earned good money at work but I was not going to splurge like I was a rock star. I left that to the athletes. Some of those dudes didn't have a problem going through a cool grand a night on hoochies and liquor but I on the other hand had plans to stack my money for my future. I wasn't cheap; I was frugal.

As I was getting comfortable and ready to relax the chime of the front doorbell rang out. I got up and walked slowly to the door. I hoped that it wasn't my parents, or one of my younger siblings making a surprise visit to my house. I loved my family. I hated pop-ups. I liked my privacy.

I walked up to the panel near the door that let me see the person who was standing on the other side of the door. It was one of the great technologies of the time. I loved it.

"Shit," I exclaimed, frustrated at who was on the other side of the door. I didn't hate this person. I didn't like talking to them because they didn't know how to go home, which was across the hall.

I didn't want to be rude and I knew she saw my car outside of the building. I know what you are saying, act as if I was asleep , but that was not the way I was trained as a child. Do unto others as you want done unto you. I alternated on when I used that belief though. Let that be clear.

"Hey, Jasmine." I greeted her with a smile as I stuck my head out of the door. It was opened enough for me to stick my head out. I wanted to send a signal of not wanting to be disturbed without being completely rude.

"I'm sorry, are you busy?" she asked as she stood really close to the door. Too close for my comfort.

"A little bit." I hoped God would grant me mercy and send her back in her house. Jasmine was a friend of Ashley's and she was in a few of my classes in high school. I thought she liked me but I made a rule of not dating a friend of my sibling's.

"I'm sorry for disturbing you. I wanted to give you a message from your grandmother."

"Really?" My eyes rose in interest. She was my maternal grandmother's at-home care nurse. My grandmother was in early stages of dementia and it was so discouraging to see at times. Sometimes she remembered you and sometimes she didn't. I used to love going over to her house and spending time with her as a child, but when I came back home from college she had changed. She was frailer than I remember and her memory of me and most people was fading. I said to myself on many a day that I was going to go over and see her and sit with her, but the uncomfortable and disheartening forgetfulness she displayed at times broke my heart. It was like a light switch being constantly turned on and off.

"Yes." A smile lit up her face. She was actually a beautiful girl. I would have fucked her a long time ago if she weren't friends with Ashley. She possibly could have been my next door booty call, but alas she was my sister's close friend and you never knew what would happen with a friendship between two females. If it went south for the winter and I was seriously dating her I wouldn't want to be forced to choose between the two. I didn't need that kind of drama. "Can I come in for a minute to share it with you?"

"Yes. Sure." I opened the door and stepped back as she walked into my apartment still dressed in her SpongeBob nurse's scrubs. I instinctively watched her behind as she made her way in. I almost reached out to smack it to see it jiggle. But I didn't. I let her go on and take a seat on my living room sofa as I closed the door.

"So what did she say about me?" I inquired as soon as I sat down on the sofa right next to her. I was in close proximity of her, enough to know that she had on a Victoria's Secret fragrance that I loved. It drove me crazy. A few of the ladies I ran into at the clubs I frequented wore it and I finally inquired about it from one of them. It was a scent that drove me wild. Damn, I wanted to reach over there, pull her by the back of her neck, and aggressively tongue her down with a wet and sloppy kiss.

She's your sister's best friend, I reminded myself and concentrated on what Jasmine wanted to tell me. I know I said she was sort of an annoyance but I still would dick her down good. I had a good piece of wood and she looked like she could suck as good as a woodpecker pecked.

"She was going on and on about you and how great a guy you were and how you were so inquisitive as a child. Like at times you would visit and you all would watch public access television together and when something interesting would come on you would run and grab a pen and paper and jot down things that you wanted to know. Then after that you would go to the computer and spend hours and hours researching, looking at pictures together. She said she loved to watch how your eyes lit up and the amazement on your face. She said she loved it. She said that you were her favorite grandchild."

"Wow," I said amazement. I vaguely remembered some of that. The last time I was over there she almost said nothing. She sat there and looked at the television or hummed a tune, which I didn't recognize, every now and then. She would smile as she looked at me from time to time, but I didn't know if that was for me or what she was watching on television. I was excited to hear that I was her favorite.

"Yes, she was smiling hard as she spoke about you. I could tell she was proud of you." Jasmine patted me on my leg. I thought my dick jumped, because she was that close or maybe I was horny. Shit, I was always horny. I shifted my leg a bit, hoping she didn't see me or it. I momentarily looked away in embarrassment.

Chapter 7

Jasmine

Delusional

Damn, is that his dick print? I wondered as I was talking to him. He had looked away for a brief second and I got a real good look at his crotch area, momentarily. It made me hot and bothered all over my body. I began to purr in my loins. He was so handsome and I knew that our children were going to look like him.

The doorbell chimed as I was about to make my move and feel up his chest and abs that showed definition through his thin-fitting T-shirt. And then I was going to show him what I wanted to do to him for oh so long.

Shit! I exclaimed in my mind. I also wanted to yell out, *Who the fuck is it?* But I didn't. I sat there and smiled. I was irritated as hell on the inside. Believe it.

He opened the door. I didn't turn to see who it was, because I had good ears. I knew it was a woman and the scent of her perfume had seeped into the room before she did. *This bitch is a booty call.* That pissed me off even more.

Pretty soon Alex invited the trick in. I stood up and got an eyeful of the ho. She was statuesque, chocolate, with a booty and ample breasts; she was a man's dream. She had pretty hair that looked like it was naturally hers but it could have been a weave. The bitch probably had a good cosmetologist or one of her other slutty friends was probably good at doing hair in the kitchen. She had on designer everything. She wasn't the average ho. She was a professional.

"Jasmine, this Ebony," Alex introduced us with an embarrassed look on his face. I wanted to tell him that there was no need to be embarrassed because she was only fulfilling a spot for the moment. She was a wet hole, like the next one that was going to slither their way up to him. *Soon, baby. Soon.*

"Jasmine is my grandmother's home healthcare provider." He looked at me and then at her. *Soon-to-be wife,* I wanted to add, but kept it cool.

"Hello, how are you?" I said as I stuck my hand out to shake hers. She did the same. Her hands were well manicured, too. I couldn't believe that Alex went for these bubblegum tricks. It made me sick to my stomach. I hoped the fake smile on my face would last, because it was threatening to turn into the frown I really wanted to give. I needed to hurry up and get the hell out of here before I fucked this bitch up for wanting to put her filthy lips on my man and future baby daddy. "That is a lovely dress you have on."

"Thank you," she said as she tugged at the bottom, trying to pull it down past her thighs.

It didn't work. Shit, she knew that she wasn't going to have that dress on for long anyway; that's why she wore it. That was a ho's requirement: easy-access pussy. I ran into these types of women all the time.

"You are rocking that haircut, baby. It is fab-u-lous."

"Thanks," I halfheartedly accepted her compliment. It was all a bunch of fake pleasantries between the both of us. She wanted my ass out and so did I. But I wanted to drag her by her hair as I left, but that wouldn't have been a good look.

There was a moment of uncomfortable silence before someone decided to speak up. So I decided to do so. "Well, let me get out of here. I have to prepare for work tomorrow." I started my way toward the door.

"Okay. Thank you for letting me know about my grandmother," Alex said as soon as we got to the door. I wanted to beg him to tell the trick to go home, but I didn't. I had plans for her.

"No problem," I said as I gave him a perky smile. He opened the door. "Nice to meet you, trick. I'm sorry, I meant Ebony," I turned and said to Ebony before I fully exited his apartment. I didn't stay turned around long enough to see the reaction on her face. But, I'm sure she knew what she was.

As soon as I closed the door to my apartment I ripped my clothes off like they were on fire. Being in his presence for that long drove me crazy. I wanted to make a baby with him right then and there. Yes, he could pump a few loads up into me. I would be fine with it. But no, he wanted to be with the ho he had over there now. It was all right. I knew she was a momentary plaything. I was going to be the wife soon enough. I was biding my time.

It didn't take long for Alex to turn on his booty call music. That enraged me more. The bitch was probably already on her knees with his meat in her mouth ready to swallow the children he was going to give me one day.

I got to my bedroom as fast as I could and pulled out the dummy that I had in my closet. It was dressed up in a tuxedo with Alex's face connected to it. I threw it on the bed and pulled out my dildo from my stash and strapped it on the dummy.

I didn't waste time; I hopped right on the bed and straddled the dummy like I was going to straddle Alex in the near future. Before I eased down on the ten inches of almost-flesh, I reached under me and adjusted the temperature of the pleasure tool. Technology was something else nowadays. I set the temperature of the dick to my pleasing. It wasn't the same as a living and breathing man underneath me, but it would have to do until such a time came. I eased down on the dick and threw my head back in pleasure.

My bedroom was close to Alex's so I could hear her moans of ecstasy. Every time she moaned I moaned right along with her, but louder. She was pleasuring Alex and so was I. Alex was giving her a real good dick down from all of the noise she was making. That pissed me off. I hopped off of the dummy, got off of the bed, and propped the dummy up against the wall. I bent over, touched my toes, and then threw my pussy back on the dildo. I fucked it until I collapsed on the floor from the orgasm Alex gave me.

I eventually got up off of the floor and made my way to the shower. I cleaned up my mess from earlier as soon as I got out of the shower. I crawled into bed with plans running through my head. Alex would be mine.

"Good night, baby." I kissed the back of Alex's head, rolled over, and went to sleep.

I shot straight up in the bed. "The bitch has got to be taught a lesson." I thought I was dreaming about torturing the bitch who was in my husband's bed.

I looked over at the clock on my dresser and it said three-fifteen in the morning. It was quiet in the building, so you heard everything at this time of night. I heard some chatter going on in the hallway. I sprinted to the front door to check to see what was going on.

"Look at this ho," I said as I watched them through my door monitoring system. My eyebrows rose in anger. She was all hugged up on Alex like the tight dress she had on.

I immediately ran back to my room and threw on some clothes and then I spied out of my window as I watched Alex walk her to her car. I quickly grabbed my keys, eased out of my apartment, and down the steps. There was waist-high, thick shrubbery that encased the building we lived in. It was enough for me to hide in and wait for Alex to go back in his apartment. After about a minute of sloppy kisses, Alex went back into the building and she got into her car and pulled off. It didn't take long for me to get to my car and follow her.

There was almost no traffic out this time of night so getting rid of her would be relatively easy. I hoped.

I shook my head as I followed her car. She was driving like she was trying to make it somewhere fast. It took us about half an hour to get into a low-class part of Baltimore City. I admit I was a little bit nervous but that didn't stop me from continuing. I kept praying that she didn't look back to see me following her. She was a terrible driver so I knew that she wasn't paying attention to me. This bitch ran stop signs and all. I kept up with her until she got to this little tore-down bar/liquor store-type of establishment that looked like all types of losers went in there. It was loathsome and very low class. There wasn't any cars around; lighting was very low in the area except for a streetlight that flickered on and off. All I could think was, *this ho is about to get liquored up right after she sexed Alex.* I guessed she couldn't live with the shame that she was a ho. I was about to help her out though.

I drove past the building and parked my car in an almost-abandoned neighborhood street about a block away. I reached in my glove compartment for my blond, long-haired front lace wig, baseball hat, shades, black gloves, and a Taser gun. I threw on the shades and gloves and grabbed the Taser gun. I looked around and made sure I was alone, grabbed my car keys, and exited my car.

For reference, this wasn't my first "fuck a bitch up" session. I had this shit with me most of the time. I switched up the wig and hat every so often to mix things up though. Alex and a bevy of hoes and yes, most of them ended up damaged goods when I finished them. Alex didn't know I was going to be his go-to wife, too, if he needed anything done. We were going to be each other's everything.

Anyway, I had on a navy blue sweat suit and black Puma tennis shoes. I was ready to handle this bitch. I stood in the shadows of the building and waited for her to make her exit back to her car. The area I was standing in reeked of alcohol and urine. I tried to breathe as little as possible as I stood there. *I'm doing this for you, Alex, baby.* I looked around a few more times making sure there were no cameras around. There was none. I heard the squeaky door of the establishment open up. She sashayed out with two black bags in hand. She was about to get tore up. But it wasn't going to be by the liquor as she hoped.

I hustled my way up to her with stealth and quickness of a cat pouncing on a mouse. She opened her car door but before she could get in I lit her up with the Taser that sent her and the liquor to the ground. I hurriedly opened the back door to her car and crammed her in. I grabbed the bags of liquor that I was glad didn't break and placed them in the passenger seat. I grabbed the keys off of the ground all while looking around and making sure the coast was clear. I hopped in the car and pulled off and around to where my car was located. I parked her car a few feet behind mines and then exited the car. I grabbed the liquor that was in the car and began to pour it all over her and the car. I was smiling the whole time. It was like Christmas for me. I know what you are saying: "All of this for a man?" Yes, bitches, all of this was for a man. Besides bitches have done far worse for one. *Ain't nobody gonna miss this ho and if she does make it out of this there is no one that will want a toasted ho.*

I grabbed a lighter out of my pocket—I was a smoker—and flicked it and threw it in the car. It didn't take long for her and her car to be fully engulfed. I looked around once again before I pulled off to make sure the coast was clear.

I made it home in about the same time it took me to get to the place I left. I felt a little guilt from what I did, but shook it off as I crawled back into bed angry that this bitch made get out of my bed to get rid of her.

Chapter 8

Troy

Dear Boy

A few days had gone by and I was now sitting in a small and quaint room where my mother was lying in the bed, high off of medication. She was on her way out. Death was knocking every day but like the soldier she was she continued to fight to live. I knew this, but that didn't stop me from coming to see her as often as I could. Others had given up but I continued to come by and sit with her. It was the least that I could do. With the murder case going on and the plotting I was doing in my head, I barely had enough time to breathe, but I made time to be here. I had to be here.

Her eyes were closed and I was sitting in a chair beside the bed watching her eyes flutter underneath her thin, closed eyelids. I wondered what she was dreaming about. The beeping monitors that were beside her bed were helping keep her "comfortable" as the nurses said to me. This was a hospice and I was told that she didn't have long. But that was many weeks ago. She said she was holding on until I completed the mission I was destined to complete.

"Is that you my dear boy? Is that you, Troy?" her low and groggy voice muttered out.

"Yes, Ma Dear. It is me, dear boy." She had called me that since I could remember and that was what I answered to when she called me. "How did you know I was here?"

She slowly turned her head toward me and then spoke; her eyes were still closed. "I heard you breathing, dear boy. You have always breathed hard. Plus, I know my dear boy. It was your time to come and see me. You are always on time to see Ma Dear." Her chest heaved upward and then back down again. A tear slid out of her left eye and cascaded down the side of her wrinkled cheek. "You loved this old woman so much. You were so faithful to me. I love you, dear boy."

"I love you too, Ma Dear." I reached over and gently grabbed her frail hand. She gripped my hand as tight as she could.

"So how are the plans going? You doing what I asked of you?"

"They are coming along quite smoothly, Ma Dear."

"I hope so. I want what is owed to me. I want . . ." She was trying to catch her fading breath.

"Calm down, Ma Dear, calm down," I said as I patted her hand. "You will see the compensation you seek. They will pay. I promise."

"Yes, make . . . them . . . pay." A few beeps of one of the machines around her started to beep louder than normal.

A nurse swiftly came to her bedside to check on her. "Is everything all right, Mrs. Martha?" She looked at her and then me. Ma Dear slowly nodded her head, but the look in the nurse's eyes said she didn't believe her.

"She needs to get some rest, sir. I need you to come back tomorrow." She looked at me sternly. I didn't object. They knew what was best for her so I rose from the chair I was sitting in, kissed Ma Dear on the cheek and then exited the room.

***

It was later this evening and I was pulling up to the Black's family residence where I was invited over for a family dinner by Ashley. It was one of a handful of times that I had been on the inside of this house. It was always warm and inviting. It was a strange feeling for me. My home wasn't quite like this one. It was . . . different.

I looked in the rearview mirror to make sure that I didn't have anything on my face. I then exited my car and walked up the well-manicured walkway. Envy enveloped me as I stood at the door getting ready to knock. The door swung open as I raised my hand to knock.

"I was wondering when you were going to come in the house. You sat in the car for a long time. I was wondering if you were having second thoughts. It's not like this is your first time here," Mona said as a warm and jovial smile covered her face. You could see where Ashley got her good looks.

"Sorry," I said as I frowned. "I had a few things on my mind."

I walked in the house and took off the blazer that I had on. She immediately took it out of my hand and hung it on the wooden coat rack by the door.

"I know the feeling. I sat in my car in front of this house a few times myself in deep thought. But don't worry; it's only temporary, whatever it is that's on your mind. Now give me a hug and join the others in the living room while I finish up this wonderful dinner we're having tonight."

"Okay," I said as I pulled away from her calming hug. I didn't want to let go. But I did, and then I made my way into living room that was a few feet away.

I quickly surveyed the room. It was filled with the entire family: Shawn, Ashley, Alex, Li'l Shawn, Diana, Ashley's youngest sister, Brittany, and Ashley's best friend, Jasmine.

Shawn, Alex, and Li'l Shawn were watching some sports on the television, while Ashley, Jasmine, Diana were engaged in conversation. Brittany was glued to an electronic gadget in her hands.

"Hey, baby." Ashley stood up and greeted me with a tight hug and a kiss on the cheek. The hug was equal to the one her mother gave me moments ago. You could tell that this family loved each other and that they were a unit. I was somewhat jealous. My family was totally dysfunctional. Ashley went back to the conversation she was in when I first arrived. I looked on in pure hate at all of them. I was a wolf among sheep.

Chapter 9

Ashley

We Are Family

Why in the hell is he looking like that, again? I thought as my younger sister, Diana, droned on and on about a guy she was dating. Troy was acting really strange lately. The look on his face hurled me back into my past like the movie of your life that flashes before your eyes in a near-death experience. It brought back so much hurt and pain that I dispersed out on so many people. He had that look of pain on his face. I heard his story, and he being in this house, full of my family, couldn't help him and the loneliness I knew he was feeling in a room filled with such love. He didn't know that this family was not always like this. This family was still a work in progress. He didn't know about us and all that we had been through. I had to do something to make him feel like he was at home. Like he could call this place home. Like he was family.

"Hold on, Diana." I put my finger up to silence her for a second. "I need to talk to Troy for a minute. I'll be right back." She gave me an agitated look but my man was more important than her puppy love at the moment. I got up and walked over to him.

"Baby, come with me for a second," I said as I grabbed his hand, not giving him a chance to say no. I pulled him upstairs and into my old room, which was now Diana's room, and then closed and locked the door. I wanted privacy like anyone else wanted.

"Baby, what's going on?" I said as we both sat down on Diana's bed. Her room was a mess. My younger siblings got away with murder, if you asked me. But that was another story for another time.

"Nothing. I am great," he said and let a smile cover his face. It was not genuine. He was hiding something.

"You sure?" I said as I gently put my hand on his cheek and turned his face toward my own. I was amazed with how affectionate I had become. I never thought I would be in this space at this time.

"Yes, I am positive." He chuckled a little. It eased my worry but I was not 100 percent confident he was being honest.

I grabbed his hand into my own. "Troy, I know that this is not something you are used to, being around my family and all, since you have so little family. I want you to know that my family is in love with you. They think the world of you. I do as well. I am so glad you came into my life when you did, because I was so unsure of myself and life in general. You mean the world to me." I couldn't believe the words that were coming out of my mouth. I was getting soft and I wasn't sure that I liked it. I was genuine in my words to him though it was new to me.

"Wow," he said with a shocked look on his face. There was some silence before he spoke again. "I don't know what to say," he said and paused again.

I was hoping that he would reciprocate the feelings toward me, but I knew that I was asking for a lot at this moment. I hoped I didn't pressure him into having to say something back. I wanted genuine feelings back as well.

"It's all right," I said as I patted his leg. "Take your time and get used to this family. We are not perfect but we love hard."

"I can see that." He smiled. This time I could feel his sincerity. "Truthfully, I was feeling a little overwhelmed from this case at work. You know this is my first case as a detective."

I nodded my head with understanding. "I believe in you. You are going to get this solved and move up the ranks yet again. You are a superior thinker and a diligent man. You got this."

"You know it is so nice to have a lady on my side. Especially a beautiful lady as yourself."

I blushed and then said, "You are trying really hard to get in my pants with all of this sweet talk." I reached over and touched his face once again. It was warm to the touch. My hand then made its way down toward his manhood. He then reached over and fondled my breast in his hand. It didn't take long for us to be in a lustful lip lock in my sister's bed. It wouldn't be the first time I did something naughty on this bed since it was the same one I slept and masturbated on in my youth.

"You are so soft and beautiful," Troy cooed as he stopped kissing me momentarily. We hadn't gone all the way but I knew that I wanted him to be my first. I was nervous because this was my first time with a man. I'd watched porn, but I still didn't know what to expect when it came to sex with a man. A dildo or a woman with a strap-on wasn't the same I'd heard.

"Thank you," I said as my breath was beginning to become shallow. He hadn't even touch me down below and I was already moist. "It's yours for the taking."

All of a sudden he pulled away.

"What's wrong?" I instantly sat up and looked at him in disappointment.

"This is not the place for this. This is your parents' house. This is not where I want to be intimate with you at." He had a serious look on his face that threw me. It was like bursting an air-filled balloon.

I felt a little bit of rage building up in me. It felt familiar. I wanted to be in control. I was used to being in control. I didn't do rejection well. It was a negative trait that I was working hard on suppressing.

"Look . . ." He placed his hand on my thigh. I wanted to push it off in anger, but I hesitated and waited to see what he was going to say. "I don't want you to think that I don't want you. I want so much from you. You don't know what you mean to me as well. I want the setting to be right."

"I understand," I said, still a little pissed. I knew that it would go away with time. "You caught me off guard."

There was a knock on the door that interrupted our moment.

"Yes," I called out.

"Mommy said for you all to come downstairs for dinner," my little sister, Brittany, said from the other side of the door. I got up, straightened my slightly disheveled clothes, and then opened the door. The look on her face was one of curiosity.

"Tell her we will be down there shortly." I gave her a "go back downstairs" look. She interpreted the look very well and turned on her heel to make her way back downstairs.

I turned and faced Troy. "Maybe you are right because I would have been really pissed with my ten-year-old sister disturbing us as we got busy." I laughed and so did he.

We both made sure we went to the bathroom and checked to make sure that we looked like we weren't making out upstairs.

As soon as we got downstairs and into the dining room, all eyes were on us.

"What?" I said as I looked around the room at everyone sitting at the table waiting for us.

"I'm glad we sent Brittany up stairs when we did. Who knows what we would have interrupted," my father said as he looked at me and then Troy. I was instantly embarrassed.

"Yes, please don't make me a grandmother yet. I still got a few good years left in me. I am not trying to sport a rocking chair yet." My mother laughed and then my father joined in on the laughter. Pretty soon everyone was laughing. Troy was laughing harder than anyone else who was in the room. I knew that he was beginning to feel like family and it made me feel good on the inside.

The rest of the night went on without a hitch and we all enjoyed ourselves as we played a few family games and then left to go to our respective homes. On the drive home I couldn't help but think about what my father and mother said about being made grandparents earlier than they wanted to be. I was not trying to be a mother before I was ready so they better know that I was going to have Troy strap up when the time came.

Chapter 10

Alex

Person of Interest

I had been home from work for about an hour and a half now. I took a small nap and now it was around five o'clock in the evening. I was lying in bed, with the television on, thinking about sex. Yes, I was addicted to it. Since I had that work done on my little soldier I was banging broads like there was no tomorrow. I was surprised I didn't have any kids yet. I always strapped up but you never know, as condoms are only 99 percent effective. Shit, my mom told us that was how Ashley and I were here today. She was on birth control when we were conceived. We were that 1 percent proof when it came to most contraception. There is always a chance to get pregnant. Always.

I was glad I didn't have any children anyway. I wasn't ready for all of that. I still had a few years of wildness in me. I turned over and reached onto the nightstand where my phone was charging. I pulled up my contact list and scrolled through looking for my next hit. I usually didn't like to hit the same broad twice but tonight I needed a quick set of warm lips, pussy, mouth, or both wrapped around my prick to bring it on home and then they went home. I didn't do overnight stays. That was a no-no. *Chicks be thinking you're in a relationship if you roll over and go to sleep and let them go to sleep. Nah, get that ass up off the floor, bed, or wherever I fucked you, get dressed, and get it moving.* I knew it seemed callous but I wasn't. I was a gentleman most of the time. I treated a woman right while they were in my company or before getting here, with maybe dinner or a movie. Most chicks knew the deal anyway. At least the ones I dealt with. Most of them wanted to get laid with no commitment as much as I did. I had a few who wanted to hang on to the dick like a monkey on a tree branch and it was understandable. I was working with a good piece of equipment.

I was flipping through my phone when something on the television screen caught my eye. It was the news. Actually the reporter. I rarely watched it and I don't know how it was even on the channel. I searched through my disheveled sheets to find the remote. I was a wild sleeper and I must have slept on the remote, which inadvertently turned it to this channel. I turned up the volume to hear what the bombshell reporter had to say:

"As of late there has been a string of unsolved female murders in Baltimore City that has police baffled. A series of young women have been found in various parts of the city in some way mutilated and unrecognizable without dental records being sought out. Police are left with little evidence to go on as the person or persons committing these heinous crimes are cleaning up their tracks very well. Names haven't been released on any of the victims at this time. Here I stand today next to the scene where a few days ago a vehicle was set ablaze with a women inside on this almost-desolate block of a lower-class neighborhood. As usual there are no witnesses in this incident. Police are urging anyone who has any information on this case to give them a call at the number that is located on the bottom of your screen. This is Jennifer Fletcher for Channel Two News."

I shook my head and flipped the channel to something that wasn't so depressing. After that I turned my attention back toward my phone and the chick I wanted to call over for a quick romp in the sheets.

It wasn't long before I had a chick over and I was blowing her back out while playing me some old-school R&B music. There was nothing like some Keith Sweat to get a chick to let you fuck her on the floor with legs wrapped around your neck as your try to send her ass to the emergency room. I got my nut and sent the chick on her way like the last one. I showered, fixed me a Marie Callender's pot pie, and climbed into bed to get some rest for the next day.

I felt good as I got up the next morning. There was nothing like a good nut, a meal, and a restful night of sleep. I put on one of my favorite suits and walked out of my apartment feeling like a million bucks.

I hopped in my car and as I was about to back my car out of its parking spot a police car pulled in back of me blocking me in.

"Ah shit, not today," I grumbled as I placed my car back in park and put on the emergency break. "What the hell do they want?" I didn't mean to have an attitude but I hoped that this was not about any petty shit like one of my neighbors reporting me for my loud music or some foolishness. This was a condo community and these pricks gave me grief about everything. I rolled down the window on my side of the car and waited to be addressed by whomever.

"Good morning, sir. Are you Alex Black?" A slender African American female cop asked after she approached my car window. I almost hit her with, "Depends on who wants to know," but I knew that may have escalated the situation to somewhere I didn't want to go.

"Yes, ma'am. I am he," I said as I smiled at her. I didn't want to give off any type or sign of tension. Tasting cement was not how I wanted to start my day.

"Mr. Black, you are needed down at the police station for some questioning." She looked at me in the eyes.

I didn't flinch. "On what matter?" I countered.

"That is not up for discussion at this present locale. The sensitivity of this matter needs to be handled behind doors." This time she smiled after she talked. I was confused.

"I can say no to this can't I?" I asked already knowing the answer.

"Yes, you can." She nodded her head. "But I don't think you want us to show up again at your place of work and bring on you a reputation that is misleading, do you?"

This mofo was good. "Okay, I do know my rights but I am going in on a voluntary basis."

"We appreciate your cooperation in this matter. We will allow you to follow us to the precinct. Don't make us regret it."

"No problem," I said and then rolled up my window and prepared to follow them to the station.

Fifteen minutes later I was sitting in an interrogation room with one of those double mirrors on one side of the room. I was at ease because I knew that I wasn't guilty of anything. I wasn't a delinquent in any form of the word. Everything in me was screaming to call my father and have him come down here to sit in this questioning with me, but I didn't want to seem like a spoiled brat who needed to call his father at the slightest problem. He had taught me enough about law that I could handle myself in this type of situation. If it got too big for me then I knew I would call, but only if need be.

It wasn't long before two officers walked into the room and greeted me. One was a regular cop type of guy; the other happened to be my sister's boyfriend, Troy. He was cool peoples to me and I knew that I was in good hands now. I played it cool and acted as if I didn't know him so that things would go smoothly.

"Good morning, Mr. Black. I'm pretty sure you don't know why you are down here this morning, but I want you to know that you have nothing to worry about. This is all routine questioning." The officer I didn't know spoke to me with a glint of doubt in his eyes. I knew the look all too well. I was a master at it as a kid and now that I was an adult I could spot it dead on. He had already convicted me in his head.

"Good morning," I spoke back, solemnly.

"Well, let's cut to the chase and get right down to business. There has been a string of murdered females in the last couple of months in Baltimore City. Have you heard about them?"

"In passing, yes," I answered.

"Well, there have been some gorgeous women being murdered and mutilated over the last month," he repeated himself. "Some pretty gruesome stuff I might add. Ferocious and very little evidence. Here are some pictures."

He slid a few pictures of some very beautiful girls over in front of me. On one side was a picture of them alive and the other side was of them deceased. I almost cringed but I held it in. I had slept with at least three of these chicks. Now I was thinking it was time to call my father.

"Mr. Black, how do you feel when you look at those pictures of those women and their mutilated bodies?" Troy finally came over and asked. He had a very serious look on his face. He was standing in the corner of the room paying attention to me before he came over to ask this question.

"How am I supposed to feel?" I countered with another question. I know it wasn't the thing to do, add tension, but hey I was not going to be forced into my feelings.

"This is not a game, Mr. Black. This is some serious shit here. Stop playing with us." Troy's voice escalated after every sentence and then he banged on the table with one of his fists at the end of the rant. It caused me to jump a little. It was definitely time to call my father.

"I know all about games. I want to call my lawyer. He'll answer all the questions about my feelings when he gets here." I looked at both of them and smiled. I had never seen Troy in this light. He was so aggressive and firm. A total opposite of what he was in a personal setting. I guessed he was doing his job.

"Look, we don't need to call any lawyers down here. These are just questions. Everybody calm down," the other officer interjected as he looked at me and then at Troy.

"I don't have a problem with questions," I said. "I have a problem with forced questioning and wordplay. You know what I mean: beating around the bush."

"Mr. Black, you are here today because three of these women had your phone number in their call logs on the night of their murders and in two you were the last call to or from. Do you have an alibi for these nights in question?" the "nice" officer asked me as he slid a piece of paper over toward me.

"These were a few girls I met through mutual friends. They were 'hit it and quit its.'"

"Excuse me, what does that mean?" the nice officer asked.

"We had sex and then they left." I broke it down to him in plain English.

"Oh, okay." He nodded his head. "So these weren't long-term relationships?"

"No." I shook my head. I was a little embarrassed because Troy didn't know that I was a ho.

"So you had no emotional ties to these women?" He asked another question.

"None, because both parties knew what the rules were. We both wanted sex and that was it. They left my house after we finished and that was the last I saw of them."

"Okay, we are going to need some alibis for these nights in question. Can you provide them?" the nice officer asked. Troy stood and looked at me with his arms folded. I wasn't sure if he was believing anything I said. I didn't care really. I was innocent and I knew it.

"Mr. Black, we are going to release you today, but we will need those alibis as soon as possible so that we can clear you as a person of interest. Okay?"

"Sure, no problem." I nodded my head.

"You are free to go," he said as he got up out of his chair and so did I.

I was out of the precinct in no time and on my way to work. During the drive I texted Troy to ask him why he treated me with such hostility in the precinct. He said that it was protocol and not to take it personal. I had assumed that but I had to text and make sure. I also would have to make up a good lie to tell my boss for my reason for being late. Confirming my alibi was going to be a task. But I knew the first person I was going to ask.

Chapter 11

Jasmine

Needy

I couldn't believe it. I just couldn't believe it. I mean I knew that it was going to happen sooner or later but I could say I was shocked to be sitting back on Alex's couch and at his request. Rewind about fifteen minutes ago and this was how the scene went down:

I was in my apartment lying across the bed daydreaming about my life-to-be when my front doorbell chimed. It startled me because I didn't get many visitors. I didn't have many friends. Anyway, I got up and made sure that I looked okay to be answering the door. I had no clue as to who it was.

To my surprise, it was Alex standing on the other side of the door. I instantly perked up and opened the door. "Everything okay?" I asked with much concern in my voice. He had a slight frown on his face.

"Yes, I need you," he said with a smile on his face. Damn, he had nice smile.

"I need you too," I slipped up and said it back to him. I wanted to bang my head up against the doorpost for being so stupid.

"Huh?" He looked at me in bewilderment.

I was so pissed that I began to mumble to myself.

"Are you okay?" he asked me with even more confusion on his face.

"Yes, I'm sorry. I am having a rough day." I tried to smile as hard as I could so it would distract him from the fool I made of myself.

"That's understandable." He smiled back. His smile made me quiver on the inside. He was so damn fine. I wanted to jump on him right here and now and give him the goodies between my legs. "I need to talk to you for a minute. Can you come over to my place for a few? I need your help."

"Sure." I nodded my head. Holding back my excitement was really hard. "Could you give me a few minutes to get decent and then I can come over?"

"Yes, sure." He then turned and went into his apartment and I closed the door to my own.

I then ran over to my loveseat and grabbed a pillow and screamed into it with all of my might as if I was a teenage girl dealing with some puppy love. I could feel my dreams coming true.

After about another quick minute I was in bathroom freshening up and then in my closet putting on my best outfit. I exited my apartment and stood in front of his door. My adrenaline was through the roof. I pushed the button on his door to alert him of my presence and it didn't take long before he was standing with the door open and his mouth open as well.

"Hey." I gave him a shy and innocent smile and batted my eyelids. I was giving him everything.

"Wow. You look . . ." He didn't even finish his statement because he was so caught up in my appearance. I had on some pink coochie cutter Victoria's Secret sleeping shorts and a midriff matching shirt that came down about an inch or two past my cleavage. I never dressed this way in public and all he saw me in most of the time was my scrubs or some regular street wear.

"Thank you." I smiled again and then tugged at my shirt as if I was trying to make it stay, covering my ample breasts. They jiggled and he smiled as he looked at them lustfully.

"You said you needed me." I reminded him of his request and my dream that was now becoming a reality.

"Yes, I . . . did," he said trying to stay focused on my face. "Come in. Come on in." He finally stepped back and let me in his apartment.

So here I was now waiting for him to come back in the room. He said he had to use the bathroom, but I knew that his dick was swollen from the outfit that I had on. He had to go in there and calm that bad boy down. I wouldn't be surprised if he squeezed out a nut while he was in there. *"I am woman, hear me roar."* I laughed at that one myself. It didn't take him long to make his way back into the room and I could tell that it was hard to control himself around a beautiful woman. He shifted himself around a couple of times as he sat on the couch with me. I was on one side of the couch and he was on the other, but I could tell he wanted to be closer. He wanted to fuck my brains out right here on this couch. I knew it. I could feel it.

"So what's the problem?" I asked as I looked intently into his eyes.

"The problem?" he said like he had no clue as to why I was in his apartment and on his couch with my pussy damn near hanging out. From the way he was looking at me I may have involuntarily left some of my juices right there on the couch. He was turning me on by the way he was looking at me. It was pure lust in his eyes.

"Oh, yeah. Damn, I lost my train of thought for a moment."

"That happens," I replied and tugged at my shirt again.

"I need you to do me a huge favor." His monster was growing in his pants and I was hoping he wanted to start working on our family right now. He saw me look but he continued with what he was saying. "I need you to be my girlfriend."

"Excuse me?" I looked at him in false bewilderment. I almost stripped down out of the little that I had on to rock him to sleep better than his mother ever could.

"Yes, I need you to be an alibi for me."

"Alibi?" I asked.

"Yes, a couple of chicks I screwed ended up dead and I was the last to be with them before they got murdered. The cops had me down at the station and everything." He shook his head. I could see a twinkling of fear in his eye. He looked desperate.

"They deserved it. I mean, how could they accuse you of such a thing? You are not that type of person." I needed to get myself together. I was slipping up too much.

"I know, right." He nodded his head. I was so glad he didn't pay that slip-up any mind.

"So what do you need me to do?" I asked, bubbling with joy on the inside.

"I need you to go down to the station with me and act like I was with you on the days after I was with those chicks. I also need you to keep this between us. My sister and my family don't need to know about this. You okay with that?"

"Sure, that is what friends are for."

"So what can I do for you to return this favor?" he asked.

"Oh, don't worry about it. It's the least that I can do for a friend."

"Now that is what I like to hear. I am so glad I can count on you for this. And I will find a way to pay you back for this."

"Aww, that is so sweet, but you really don't have to. Let's hope you return the favor when I need it. Let me know when we have to go down to the station and I will be by your side."

"Again, thank you so much," he said as he got up from the side of the couch he was on. I did the same.

"I guess I'll see you later," I said as I made my way to the door. Everything in me was hoping that he came up behind me and forced his tongue down my throat but that did not happen.

I left his apartment and walked into my own with some more plans on my mind. I was so glad that my man was coming to his senses. Who knew that murdering a couple of bitches for him would cause him to get closer to me? I hoped that he left them shady broads alone and then I wouldn't have to kill those bitches. Maybe he would be leaving them alone for good and now I could make my move on him so we could be the happy couple that we were supposed to be.

I went to bed a happy camper. I almost couldn't sleep because of my nagging mother's voice. I took me a sleeping pill, covered my head with a pillow, and drifted off into la-la land.

Chapter 12

Troy

Moving Forward

I sat at my desk trying to think of a way to get Alex dismissed as a suspect from this case. It wasn't because I thought he was innocent. I didn't give a fuck about his innocence or guilt. I had plans for him and I didn't want the system to get him before I did. He owed my family some blood and I was going to get him and his sisters if it was the last thing I did. I'd been waiting and waiting for this opportunity and now that it was here I wasn't going to let it or anything stop me from stopping this bloodline from ruining any more lives. I had to do this. I promised that I would. I was groomed for this very task.

I had finished high school early, enrolled into the police academy soon after, and excelled until I was promoted to a detective a few months ago. This was my first major case and my superiors assigned me because of my exemplary record with the force in these last four years. I was a decorated officer early on and was hated by many in the precinct where I was stationed. I didn't take any bullshit and I didn't give any out. I wasn't here to make friends. I was there to get a job done and to protect and serve. Yes, I had my own agenda going on but I took my discipline as a hardworking individual seriously. My life was fucked up early on and I was pushing ahead to clean up the mess.

It wasn't long before there was a knock on my office door. One of the front desk officers escorted Alex Black and Ashley's best friend, Jasmine, into the office. I didn't know but there was something about Jasmine that made me a little curious about her. She was different and I couldn't really put my finger on what it was that was different about her.

"Good afternoon, Mr. Black," I said as I stood up out of my chair to greet him. I greeted him as if I didn't know him. It was easy, because again, I couldn't stand him. He resembled bad blood to me like his other two siblings. All three were going to pay. *Wait and see.*

"Good afternoon, Detective Lee." He reached out to shake my hand. I masked the disdain for him behind a smile.

"Please take a seat." I pointed to the two chairs in front of my desk as I closed the door to my office. I then walked back to my desk and took a seat. "What can I do for you today?"

"I'm following up with my alibi for those dates you asked me about a few days ago." He looked confident in every word he spoke. It was a quality that all three of them had: confidence. It made me furious on the inside. My leg was shaking uncontrollably underneath my desk.

"Okay." I looked at him waiting for his proof.

"Well, on those three days I was with my girlfriend and she can vouch for my whereabouts. Right, baby?" He reached over and grasped Jasmine's hand into his.

"Yes, my baby was with me all night long." Jasmine smiled from ear to ear. I had to admit she was a very attractive woman. But again, something was off with her. I could feel it.

"So you are saying that you know that he was sleeping with these women and he would come home to you? You know about this?" I looked at her intently waiting for any glitches of a lie being told.

"What?" She looked at him as outrage instantly flared up in her. I was amazed at how fast her temper rose. Then all of a sudden she reached back and slapped him. The look on his face was of pure shock. "You was with some bitches before you came over my house. You said they were clients. You lied to me? How could you do this to me?" She stood up and went for the door.

Alex immediately rose out of his chair. "Baby, wait, I'm sorry. I never meant to hurt you." He walked up to her and tried to touch her, but she pushed him away.

"Don't touch me." Her head quickly snapped in his direction. "You said this wouldn't happen again. You said she wouldn't hurt me again." Tears streamed down her face one after the other.

"Baby, please. It won't happen again. I mean it this time." He was damn near begging her.

I was actually enjoying the show.

"I don't know." She turned toward him with a frown on her face. "You promise?"

"Yes, I promise," he said as he eased over to her until she voluntarily accepted his embrace. She melted up into his arms. Pretty soon they were kissing passionately. So much so that I was getting aroused. I cleared my throat to get their attention.

"Excuse me; I don't want to be rude." I looked at both of them emotionlessly. "But I need you, Jasmine, to sign an affidavit to all that you are saying. Are you willing to do that?"

"Yes, I am," she said as she freed herself from Alex's embrace and they sat back down in front of me.

"Okay, let me get my tape recorder and paperwork ready. I will need to state the dates and location that you both were together and then sign a few pieces of paperwork and you two lovebirds can be on your way."

They both smiled and nodded in agreement.

After about an hour Jasmine and Alex were out of my office and I was documenting some more notes to show to my boss before I left for the day. I was shocked to know that those two were even in a relationship. They didn't act like it when we were around each other. I planned on inquiring to Ashley about it even though I really didn't care.

When I got off of work I had to visit Ma Dear and then it was on to a date with Ashley. I was feeling good because I had things going the way I wanted them to go. Payback was hard to fulfill, but rewarding to say the least. I wouldn't be completely happy until their blood was running out of their lifeless bodies like a running faucet.

Chapter 13

Ashley

The Ill Na Na

A few days had passed and I was so excited about having dinner with Troy tonight. I was so excited about this relationship. It was so promising. I could see me marrying him and starting a family with him. Sure, he had his moments, but I was willing to look past them because I had my own issues going on as well. I thought tonight was the night I was going to tell him about my past. I wanted to continue this relationship with honesty like he did with me. No more lies.

I was sitting at a nice, charming table in the back of a restaurant that was sophisticated and classy. It had white tablecloths, candles, soft music playing, and low lighting to give off a romantic ambiance. It was enchanting as I looked around the room at the twelve or so tables that were spread out across the room. It was an adult atmosphere. I was still in disbelief that I was even in a setting like this one without causing a scene or something. I was a scene maker for sure. Well, at least I *was* a scene maker. I had grown up some and I was quite proud of my reserved attitude. I was wondering if it was a lasting change or one that I had forced onto myself. Well, time would tell.

Troy had texted me a few minutes ago letting me know that he was running late but he was on his way. He was caught up in traffic on I-695. Traffic on I-695 could be problematic if you caught it at the wrong time of day or if an accident occurred. I knew that he wouldn't be here for at least another fifteen or twenty minutes. It was all right with me because I was loving this place and the wine that I ordered was keeping me good company. I loved being an adult. I closed my eyes and enjoyed the moment. I even swayed in my seat a bit.

My moment of solitude was interrupted by a tap on my hand that was calmly sitting on the table. My eyes popped open and then I closed them again hoping that I was dreaming.

This couldn't be happening. This had to be my karma or something. I couldn't believe it. *Shit! Shit! Shit!* I screamed in my head.

I slowly opened up my eyes to the reality before me. "Antoinette," I spoke as dryly as I possibly could. I wanted her to know that she was not welcome here, at all. But then I looked at her attire. It was a chef's uniform. This bitch, excuse me, woman, worked here. This was her place of employment. *Ugh!* I would have thought that since this was well outside the city limits I wouldn't run into anyone I knew or who knew of me, but alas, here I was with a run-in in front of me.

"I was having a rough day until I came out here for a break, looked across the room, and saw you." She was smiling like the Cheshire cat.

It made me sick to my stomach.

"You a sight for sore eyes, girl. Ump, ump, ump." She leaned over and looked me up and down from the side. "Your ass spilling out of that seat you in."

It made me feel creepy. "Really?" It was rhetorical, but I knew this bitch, I mean woman, was going to misinterpret it any way I said it to her. She was causing me to revert to my old ways. *This is what happens when your past shows up all of a sudden and catches you off guard. They want to drag you backward. No, sah, not today!*

"Yeah, girl." She smiled hard, again. "You got that ill na na." She even danced a little in her seat to the beat that was probably playing in her head.

Truth was it played a little in my head as well. But I moved past the moment because I wanted her to move on past this one. "Antoinette, this is not the time for this. Actually, there is no time for this." I looked at her with as much seriousness as I could muster up. I was hoping that she got the point and moved on graciously and with haste.

"Oh, you out on a date?" She looked at me with a little surprise on her face. "You got you a little bitch you about to work over tonight? Y'all want some company? I can't promise I won't dominate the scene but I can't wait to taste you again."

"What!" I looked at her in shock. Every part of that statement was crazy. She looked crazy saying it. Her ass had to be about fifty-five or older. Who in the hell was she going to toss up? "Are you serious?"

"You remember the way I used to do you. I know that you do. There is no denying that you liked it." She looked at me hoping I was going to bite the bait she was feeding me called memories. This piece of fish wasn't biting.

"Antoinette, where are we at now?" I asked her.

"Huh?" She looked dumbfounded. "We at my job."

"No, boo, we are in the present. You know, the right now. And right now I am not trying to hear any of that. I am glad you have your memories. Try licking on those for old times' sake. Because you will never taste me again."

"Oh, so it's like that." She sat up straight and leaned back farther away from me.

"I've been trying to be nice to you, but you weren't trying to take the hint. I'm not on that side of the street anymore, if you get my drift."

"Oh, really." She had an even more shocked look on her face now.

"Yes, really." I twisted my lips up giving her the "now get the fuck on" look.

"Hey, baby, who's this?" Troy said as he walked up to the table, catching us both off guard.

"Oh, ahhh. This is . . ." My voice trailed off as I looked at Antoinette. "This is a friend of mine."

"Friend?" Antoinette got up and looked at me and then Troy. "We were more than that." She cocked a slick smile on her face.

"Huh?" Troy looked at her and then me in confusion. I wanted to melt like the Wicked Witch in *The Wizard of Oz*.

"Girl, stop playing." I reached out and playfully pushed her on the shoulder.

"I'm not playing." She looked at Troy. "She didn't tell you that she liked pussy?"

"Huh?" Troy looked at me confused. I wanted to punch this bitch straight in her mouth. But I kept my cool.

I opened my mouth but nothing came out to explain the situation that I was currently in. This was not supposed to go down like this. I so wanted to tell him myself and not have it come to him like it was right now. Yeah, karma was definitely a bitch named Antoinette.

"Yeah, man, I'm surprised you didn't see my name tattooed across that twat of hers. I licked her so much she probably still got my tongue print down there. I used to have her twisted up worse than two wrestlers in a ring." She laughed as she said that.

Troy looked at me, waiting for me to say something. I did something that I never did before. I bitched up and I ran. To the bathroom that is. As soon as I got to the bathroom, I checked to see if anyone else was in there with me. After I made sure I was alone, I locked the door. I didn't know how I was going to show my face again. The look of pure shock on Troy's face was etched in my mind. He looked like a deer caught in some headlights. Antoinette's face showed pure satisfaction. I wanted to crawl out of the restaurant on my hands and knees to escape Troy or my truth that was spilled all over that table. But, my purse was still at the table. I was pissed at myself for not grabbing that before I stormed off. But this whole messed-up situation didn't allow for any thinking. Just me hauling ass out of there. That was the first time in my life that I ran from anything. I mean I hid some stuff but I didn't run from anything. I caused people to run, but now the table was turned and here I was huddled up in a bathroom stuck on stupid.

There was a knock on the door. I hoped it wasn't someone who really needed to go to the bathroom because she was going to be a pissy or shitty mess waiting for me to come out.

There was another knock on the door letting me know that the person wasn't going away.

"Ashley," Troy's voice called out from behind the door. I tensed up and got quiet. Maybe he would go away.

There was another knock. "Ashley, I know you are in there. Come on out so we can talk. I'm not mad at you. Come out and talk."

The muscles in my body started to relax. I was still afraid though. Afraid of what he thought of me. Was he going to stop dating me after this? Was he going to believe anything else I said after today? *Ashley, get yourself together. It wasn't a lie. You didn't tell him everything. You left out some stuff. People do it all of the time.*

"Right," I said as I looked at myself in the mirror. "We can get past this."

I walked over to the door, unlocked it, and then opened it. Troy was standing there with a smile on his face. "Hey."

"Hey," I said back trying to continue to look into his eyes as he did me.

"Let's go back to the table. We can salvage this." He pulled me by the waist, close to him, and kissed me on the lips.

We slowly separated and I looked at him in his eyes. "Okay."

It was the first time I felt good not being in control. It felt fabulous.

As we made our way back to the table, me in front of him, there was no one staring at us. I was amazed because I was sure somebody in the restaurant heard the incident.

We took our seats and he looked at me for a few moments before he spoke again. I didn't really have anything to say. I was still in a vulnerable place right now.

"Ashley, you have nothing to be ashamed of. We all have a past. My thoughts of you have not changed at all."

"I don't know what to say." I looked at him with tears threatening to fall. I was pissed that I was being this emotional right now. This was definitely a first for me.

"You don't have to say a thing. It's behind us. We are moving forward," he reassured me. The look in his eyes was sincere. It moved me on the inside.

I was speechless once again. This moment was too unreal. All this emotion and drama was too much for me at the moment.

"Tell you what, let's get out of here and go to another restaurant before anything else happens in here. I want to enjoy the rest of the day. It was quite eventful enough for the both of us." He laughed and I let a smile open up onto my face.

The rest of the night was uneventful and both went our separate ways afterward. He called to make sure I got home safely and then it was the shower and to bed for me. A good night's sleep was needed for me.

Chapter 14

Alex

Dilemmas

I was sitting at my desk after I got off an important call for one of my clients and I couldn't help but flash back to a couple of days ago when I was in the police office with Jasmine. She really put on a performance. We had done no rehearsing or any of that. It was all improvisation. At the beginning when she slapped me, I was about to slap her ass back though. That shit hurt like hell. But I kept my composure and moved ahead with it. At the end when I kissed her and she stuck her tongue in my mouth, also unplanned, I wanted to take her ass somewhere and fuck the shit out of her for that one. She was definitely a firecracker. I could see why she and Ashley were friends, even though Ashley had calmed down quite a bit over the last year or so. But again, Jasmine was Ashley's friend and didn't want to go down that path. I reached down and grabbed my dick through my pants and squeezed it. I was envisioning me banging her back out in my mind.

The nasty thoughts were instantly snatched from in front of me when there came a knock at my door. I didn't have an appointment for anybody to show up at my office so I was kind of pissed off at the interruption. I was primed to take my monster out and "suicide" a few of my sperm into one of them Kleenex on my desk.

It could be that receptionist coming in to get a piece of this wood she was avoiding this last couple of days. She knew she wanted to slide down this pole. I instantly perked up and said, "Come in."

One of my high-earning professional football players walked in. He had a look of nervousness on his face.

"Hey, Lance. What can I do for you?" He was a strapping guy. All muscle and testosterone. All the ladies wanted him but he was a married man with five children. He was only thirty-two years old. I could only assume that he broke a few headboards in his life by his stature. His wife would probably fight in the street to hang on to him. Some of this he told me but some was speculation as well.

"I'm in some deep shit," was the first thing he blurted out of his mouth.

I got up out of my chair and closed my door. As I walked back to my desk all manner of things popped into my head. What in the hell could he have gotten himself into that would make him come here?

"And you came here?" I looked at him, curiously waiting for him to spill the news that he was holding on to. "I'm only your agent." I did handle some of his personal affairs but not many. I was more of his business agent. I mostly got him endorsement deals and the like. His wife and his lawyer was on top of his money. He was a cool guy and all of that, but I wasn't sure if I wanted to know what he was holding on to. I partied with a few of them but I didn't want to know any secret or get caught up in no shit that would cause me to lose my job or my credibility. Yes, I was a little loose at times, but I did my best to keep my business life clean. Everyone had a slip-up every now and then.

"I know, man. You seem like a trustworthy guy. I need to run something past you to get your advice."

"Okay," I said as I scooted closer to my desk so I could listen more attentively.

"I got this situation man that I can't control. My wife/ accountant got my money on lock. My PR person is my holier-than-thou cousin. You're the only one I can trust. And I need some serious advice on this."

"Whatever we talk about will stay between us," I reassured him. It was actually true. Agents had to sign a disclosure agreement when you signed on to this agency.

"Okay." He paused for a long time. I waited patiently though. I was still the nosey twin. Believe that. "I went out to this private type of whorehouse to get me some freaky stuff done to me. It was a place that specialized in keeping your identity a secret." He looked at me as he talked.

I nodded my head in understanding.

He continued, "Okay, so I'm in there getting my freak on and drink on. Now here is the problem: somebody slipped something in my drink. I woke up the next morning in a bed all alone. All I can remember is this chick with this banging-ass body work her magic on me before I took this drink. That it." He placed his head in his hands and then started rubbing his face in anguish.

"So, what's the problem?" I asked, disappointed at the fact that what I heard wasn't as juicy as I thought it would be.

"I gathered my shit and got the hell out there. I was a foggy mess, man. My head was spinning and shit. I was fucked up. But that's not the kicker. As soon as I got in my car and pulled off, I got a text with an attachment to it. Here take a look at it." He took his phone out of his pocket and slid it over to me.

I pushed a few buttons and a video popped up and started playing. I watched as this pretty chick give him the blow job of his life. I mean she was putting in work.

She was dressed up in a little nurse's uniform and all. Lance looked as if he was high and enjoying the pleasure she was giving him. They both were making pleasurable noises. Then the sucking stopped abruptly and I scrolled down to another attachment. It was another video. This one was of the pretty chick doing a few selfies of herself and then placing the recording device in a stationary position and she continued to record herself as she stood in front of the camera. First she pulled off her wig and my mouth hung open in shock. Next she took off her bra exposing a flat chest. The finale was complete when she pulled down her underwear and exposed a deflated penis. I looked up at Lance with complete shock written all over my face. This was crazier than what I had watched in California a few years back. This one took the cake.

"I know." He shook his head. "Scroll down again."

I did as I was instructed and it was another video. I listened as it played:

"Hey, Lance, my name is Henry. I'm pretty, ain't I? You like my skills? I like yours. You have a real monster in them pants. I wish I could keep it. Anyway, I know you are scared as shit right now and you need to be. Because I have all of the contacts off of your phone and one press of the send button and your life as you know it is over. All I want is some money. I can't do this nasty shit all of my life, so I am going to need you to come up off of some of that dough I know you have. I knew who you were right out of the gate. That mask you had on couldn't hide that big-ass head of yours and that crooked smile you have. I almost didn't go through with it when I was giving you the head job, but then I said you fucked up the minute you crossed the seal of the door. You jocks will do anything to bust a nut. Well, you did a fifteen-year-old for that good ol' nut you got. Was it worth it? It was to me. I am going to need two million dollars to keep this video a secret. You don't have long so don't keep me waiting. I'll be in touch with the specifics later. Sleep tight." He winked and then the video faded out.

My head slowly rose up to look at Lance. I was speechless. He was fucked big time.

"What am I going to do?" He looked at me helplessly.

"Do you have any money stashed away?" I asked him.

"No, my wife has all of that on lock." He shook his head.

"Damn." I shook my head as well.

"Man, I haven't even been home yet. I am fucking screwed. All for a nut. What am I going to do?" He looked at me. I didn't have an answer for him.

"I think you might have to bite the bullet and confess this to your wife." I spoke earnestly.

"Man, I can't do that. This is not the first time this has happened. I have messed up before and she let me slide. This right here might take her over the edge. She can take all of my money and property if she catches me cheating again. She got me locked in an agreement. Man, this would ruin me if this came out. I could lose everything and do some jail time. I can't believe this shit."

"Lance, keep calm and let me talk to my dad about this situation and see what he says. There might be a chance you get out of this." I wasn't sure if what I was saying was true, but I was trying to give him some hope to cling on to. Truth was, I wasn't even sure I was going to mention this to my dad. Lance might be on his own with this one.

"Okay," he said as he got up out of the chair.

"I'll call you in a day or two. Call me if anything changes."

"I will." He looked at me with fear in his eyes. "But please keep this hush-hush, bro. I'm trusting you."

"I got you." I walked him to the door, opened it, and watched him wait for the elevator. He looked back once more as the elevator arrived and then he stepped on it.

I walked back in my office, closed the door, and then flopped down in my chair. This was quite a dilemma and I was glad for once it didn't involve me.

Chapter 15

Jasmine

Wet

"Why can't you let these tricks go? Why are you making me do this? All I wanted to do was live my life with you, have your children, and cook your food." I sat in my window and watched him walk with another chick. It was sickening to watch him grope her as they walked across the short parking lot. I didn't know where they were going but at least it wasn't inside of his home. It was late at night, about eleven o'clock at night. I hoped that he was changing his mind and taking that broad home. They had come in a little earlier that night, but there was no music playing so I could only assume that he didn't fuck her. You would have thought that he would have learned his lesson by narrowly escaping possible multiple murder charges with the help of my excellent performance skills. I gave up everything in that office for him. It was a performance that I could have gotten an Oscar for. I had broken-hearted girlfriend down to a tee. I could still taste the sweet nectar of his kiss from when he let my tongue swim around in his mouth those few short seconds. He made really wet thinking about him.

"What am I going to do with you?" I said as I continued to watch him walk her to her car and then as he walked over to his. I was hoping that he was following her to make sure she got home safely and not taking her back to her place to fuck. I was actually talking about both of them. I had to get rid of her and teach Alex about loyalty and obedience as well. He was like a dog off of his leash. I was tired of him treating me like I wasn't here waiting for him at night. And, longing for his long, wet kisses between my legs. He was pissing me off slowly but surely.

I had to handle this chick though because the police was hot on the trail of the murderer aka me. I didn't know if they were watching Alex or what. I had to stand down until the heat died down. That took me back to the police office for a minute. Troy was looking at me quite oddly. I wondered if he was on to me. Or, if he believed my performance. He looked like the regular dumb guy, you know, slow in the head. Alex was the exception though.

I was broken out of my trance by the ring of my phone. I walked over to the living room table and picked it up. "Hello," I answered with some pep in my voice.

"Girl, what are you doing?" Ashley's upbeat voice rang out through the receiver of my phone.

"Nothing at the moment," I answered.

"Well, get dressed and put on something hot. We going out to get you a man and I won't take no for an answer. I'll be there in twenty. Be outside waiting." Then the phone went dead.

I looked at the phone in disbelief. I would go out but I wasn't going to enjoy myself.

As scheduled, twenty minutes later I was on the outside of my building as Ashley pulled up in front of the door. I hopped in her car and she pulled off.

"Girl, you look hot in that dress," she said as I strapped myself in. "We are going to get you a man if it's the last thing I do." She was smiling hard. I plastered on a fake smile as best I could.

"I know that's right." I pepped up a little to fake out some more. Truth was my man was probably fucking the brains out of that bimbo right now. I wanted to open the door to the car, take a few hard rolls on the cement, and make my way back home and track my man down, but I didn't. I sat still and pretended like I was going to be all over a few lame-ass dudes wherever we were headed to. "Where are we headed to anyway?"

"To this hot club called Wet. It's new and I know we can find you at least a man for the night up in there." She laughed and I let out another fake chuckle. I was going to be doing a whole lot of faking tonight.

We pulled up to the club and there was already a line forming to get in. I wasn't really the crowd type of girl. I like being in a setting with one on one. Not a bunch of sweaty men acting like they needed to get a nut before the stroke of twelve or else their dicks would shrivel up and fall off. Men were desperate. Alex wasn't like them; he had to beat the skanks off of him. I knew that they practically threw themselves at him. That's what I was trying to save him from. He wasn't going to ever ask me for sex because if he breathed the right way I would be on my knees ready to take him in my mouth.

"You hear me, girl?" Ashley poked me in my shoulder breaking me out of thought.

"Yeah." I nodded my head.

"No, the hell you didn't. You were off in some far-off land." She laughed. "I spotted a few good-looking ones in the line already. Girl, we gonna get you somebody to come to my wedding with."

"Troy proposed?" I looked at her, shocked.

"Girl, no. But I do think he is the one." A bright smile covered her face. It was one of satisfaction.

"Really," I said with a little more gloom in my voice than there should have been. "That is so nice." Now I really wanted to go back home and track that bitch down and cut her head off.

"Yes, it is. Who would have thought that I would be in this place that I am in right now?" She shook her head. I could see a few tears welling up in the corners of her eyes. Her ass was getting soft. I remembered when she didn't even get emotional. Her ass was as close to being a guy a chick could get, emotionally wise anyway. She was still a chick, but she was tough. Now a man has softened her up.

"I know right. You was a real bitch in high school. Bitches wanted your head on a stick." I chuckled a little and then looked at her face.

Her face was stone-cold serious.

"Girl, I was joking. I mean you wasn't that bad. You was a little rough around the edges." I stammered on through the words I said. She still had the same look on her face.

Then she burst into laughter. "Girl, I was a piece of work wasn't I? I've done some crazy stuff in my past."

"Yes, but that is the past." I nodded my head.

"Okay, now let's get out of this car and get you a man."

We both got out of the car and headed across the street. I had to admit there were some good-looking guys in the crowd.

We stood in line for fifteen minutes before we were frisked and let into the club. It wasn't your typical type of club. The music was pumping but it wasn't that hood music, you know, fuck this, lick that. And there wasn't anyone dry humping on the floor. I was relieved. I wanted to find a spot and become incognegro.

"Girl, there are some eyes on you already." Ashley whispered in my ear as we made our way across the club. She was guiding me toward the bar. I wasn't really a drinker, but tonight I needed something to take my mind off of Alex and that sleazy girl he was with.

"Girl, what are you ordering?" Ashley asked me as we both sat at the bar. There were a few others sitting along the same bar. Everybody was in their own world.

"What can I get for you lovely ladies?" a black male bartender asked us.

"Something very light and fruity please," I ordered.

"Give me a Long Island Iced Tea," Ashley ordered. "Jazz, we are going to enjoy ourselves tonight. I am hoping this is the only drink I have to pay for tonight," Ashley said as she laughed. "There's nothing like a few free drinks. These fellas in here don't have to know that I'm taken until after the drink is paid for," she said as she leaned over toward me and then laughed. I did as well; again, I didn't really want any men all up on me, free drink or not. The bartender came back with our drinks moments later and we both sipped on it them for a few seconds. "Excuse me, you here with someone?" A guy came up and slid into the recently vacated seat next to me. "Or are you all alone tonight?"

I turned my head in his direction. "I'm here with my girl next to me, and she and I are chilling tonight."

"What girl?" He looked at me in curiosity. I turned my head and noticed that Ashley had vacated her seat, with her drink, without my knowledge.

"Oh, she must have gone to the bathroom or something." I smiled in an awkward manner. I really wasn't for this.

"Good." His smile showed up again.

I had to admit he was a good-looking brother but he wasn't getting any play tonight. I wasn't going to be rude though. I'd at least talk to him. Check his game. I was hoping this brother was full of himself so he could talk and talk and make this night go by faster. It was a Saturday and I had nowhere to go tomorrow.

"So what's your name, beautiful?"

"Jackie," I lied.

"That's a beautiful name." He eased a little closer to me. His hot-ass breath was permeating my space. I pulled back on the seat I was in as far as I could go, which wasn't much. "How could I get to know you better?"

"You don't want to know me." I shook my head. "I'm bad for your health."

"Sounds like a challenge." He perked up. I groaned on the inside. I turned away from him briefly to see where Ashley had gone off to when my eyes fell on a most amazing sight.

"Alex," I whispered under my breath. Now I perked up.

"Excuse me?" The guy next to me sounded confused.

"Huh?" I looked back at him.

"You said something, but I didn't hear you," he answered.

"Oh, I saw someone I knew. I have to go." I got up out off of my stool before he could say another word. I followed Alex around the club with my eyes as I made my way to a wall to blend in. The club had grown crowded in a matter of minutes. Alex was not alone. He had the same girl with him from earlier. My blood raged in my veins. I was going to get rid of her before the night was over.

"Girl, what are you doing over here by yourself?" Ashley had unexpectedly eased beside me.

"Ash, these dudes are lame. I'm not interested." I twisted my face up as I looked out into the crowd of people.

"Hey, look what we have here." Alex popped up on us as we talked. He had his side piece with him and she was all over him. I wanted to puke. "Destiny, this is my sister, Ashley, and her girl Jasmine."

I wasn't up for pleasantries at all. I tried to smile graciously. She reached out to shake our hands, Ashley's and then mine.

"Hey let's grab a table," Ashley suggested. There were only a few on the outskirts of the club. We made a beeline to the closest one that was empty of people. There was a drink on it but we sat down anyway.

"Yes, my feet are hurting in these heels, girl." Alex's girl looked at me for agreement. I really didn't want to say anything back to this trick.

"Yeah, I know what you mean." I smiled back.

"Hey, I'm about to go to the bar to get a drink; anyone want one?" Alex asked as he got up out of his chair and looked at us.

"No, I'm good," I spoke up before anyone else did, because one drink was enough for me tonight. And I didn't even get to finish that one. I was in the minority because Ashley and Destiny chimed in with their orders. A few minutes had passed before Alex had made his way back to the table where we were seated.

We sat there as the atmosphere around us went on. The music was really going now and the people thronged the floor with bodies mashing into each other. Ashley had gotten up and danced with a few guys while I watched on in boredom. She was really enjoying herself. Then the worst thing that could happen, happened. Alex and Destiny made their way to the dance floor as a freak 'em song came on. They joined in the crowd of people who were already out there getting their freak on with clothes on. I watched as she ground her ass into his crotch as if she was trying to get pregnant by him. They were dancing really hot and heavy.

"Jazz, you missing you one hell of a good time out there. I am getting my life. I am sad that Troy couldn't come with us. He said he had some work to do on a case he was on, but he said that I should have fun and enjoy myself. And I'm doing just that." She was a little tipsy from the drinks that she had drunk. She was good enough to drive home though. I hoped.

"I'm so glad that you are." A faint smile crossed my face. "I'll be ready to go home in a few. Let me go use this bathroom real quick." I got up and made my way through the people and found the bathroom deep in the back of the establishment. I walked in and there was no one in the bathroom. It was odd because ladies were always in the bathroom. I shrugged my shoulders and made my way into one of the stalls to relieve my bladder. I couldn't hold my water well. As I was finishing up in the stall I heard the door open and the music from the dance floor made its way into the bathroom momentarily. Then I could hear a set of heels going across the floor and into one of the stalls. The door shut and I exited my own. I walked up to the faucet so I could wash my hands and be on my way.

"Damn, ain't no toilet paper in this stall," the person in the stall exclaimed in frustration. I laughed to myself as I finished washing my hands.

"Excuse me, can you hand me some toilet paper?" she asked.

I stayed silent. Her ass should have checked before she squatted. Any idiot knew that shit.

"I hear the water running. I know you hear me," she bellowed again, this time with more agitation in her voice.

"Okay, hold on," I said in defeat. I didn't want to go near anybody while they were on a toilet. It was a pet peeve of my mine. The only reason I did it for my patients was because I was getting paid good money to do it. Real good money. Her ass was lucky I was in a good mood.

I walked into the stall I came out of and pulled some tissue off of the roll that was in there. I got what I thought was an adequate amount of tissue for any person and exited the stall.

"Here you go," I said as I knocked on the stall.

"Hand it to me underneath the door," she requested.

I looked down at the floor and then the door. "Baby girl, open the stall and I'll hand it to you. This place is filthy." At least it was by my standards.

"Damn, why you got to be so difficult?" She groaned but then the door to the stall opened. It was Alex's ho with her dress around her waist and her underwear around her ankles. I was shocked she had on underwear truth be told.

"Hey, girl." Her face lit up at the sight of me. You would have thought we would have known each other's voices, but shit we didn't know each other that long to care. At least I didn't. "I'm so glad you didn't leave me hanging."

"Yeah, girl. I'm real particular with my bathroom habits."

"Me too, girl."

I wanted to tell that bitch to stop lying but I kept it cool. "All right, girl, handle your business," I said as I turned and walked away from her stall. Now was my opportunity to get rid of this bitch. I walked to the bathroom door and hoped that it had a lock. All I needed was a few minutes to handle this bitch.

I took my shoes off at the door and crept back into the stall next to her hoping she didn't hear me. I looked at my watch to time myself. I gave myself five minutes to get this done. As soon as I heard her flush the toilet I readied myself for an attack.

As soon as she exited her stall I grabbed her from behind and quickly placed her in a figure-four headlock from behind. I had a real good grip on her as she tussled to break free, but the bitch was no match for me. I was a black belt and I had some incredible strength when I was in the moment. It didn't take but thirty seconds for her to go limp. I dragged her into the handicap stall and closed the door. I had to make sure this bitch was really dead. I had to think quickly. I pulled her body over to the toilet and placed her head in the bowl of the toilet. It wasn't easy because the toilet didn't have a high level of water. I pushed her head down in the toilet with my feet as I stood on top of her and used my weight to push her head down farther. I wanted to drown her but the pop I heard let me know that her neck was broken. Now that I was sure that she was dead. I hoisted her body up as best I could without touching her too much. I didn't want to leave any evidence. Anyplace I thought I might have touched I rubbed down with a piece of my clothing to smear any fingerprints. With technology the way it was nowadays I was really pushing it with that. I locked the stall and climbed over to the other stall using the handicap railing and the toilet tissue dispenser. I washed my hands again and then exited the bathroom. I made my way back to the table like I didn't just murder Alex's latest bed buddy. It was all in a good day's work.

"Girl, you ready to go?" Ashley walked up to the table and sat down next to me.

"Whenever you are ready," I answered, smiling genuinely for the first time all night.

"Okay, let me get one more dance in and then I'll be ready." She got back up and made her way back to the dance floor.

"Jazz, did you see Destiny in the bathroom while you were in there?" Alex asked me as he walked up to the table. His eyes were really glazed-looking. I could tell that he was getting close to being drunk.

"Well, I don't know how to tell you this, but as I was coming out I saw her go into the men's bathroom with a guy." I looked at him like it was hard for me to tell him this great lie.

"She was a ho anyway." He picked up his drink and took the last swig of it.

"I'm sorry that I had to tell you that. But as a friend I couldn't let you waste your time with her knowing what she had done. A real friend wouldn't do that." I reached over and put my hand on his. He looked at me and smiled.

"Jazz, you one cool girl. I'm glad you my sister home-girl."

"I am too," I agreed.

"All right, Jazz, I'm ready to go." Ashley came back to the table and sat next to me. "Alex, where is the girl you was with?"

"Her ass probably somewhere on her knees. I don't know." He looked a little pissed off. He got up from the table and staggered a bit.

"Alex, Jazz is going to drive you home. You are too drunk to drive." She looked at him and then at me. "Is that all right with you, Jazz?"

She didn't know that she didn't have to ask me to drive my man home. This was working out to be a night to remember.

"That's okay with me." I looked at her then at Alex. "Is it okay with you, Alex?"

"Yeah, girl. You can ride me home." He smiled and staggered again. His words were all I wanted to hear right not. I prayed with everything in me that I would ride him when we got home.

We grabbed our things and we had to help him get into the car.

"Jazz, you want me to follow you home so we can help him get in?"

"Nah, girl, I'll be good. He's not that heavy. If I can lift some of them heavy folks up at work I can definitely help him make it a few feet to his house."

"All right, girl," she said she started to walk away. "Text me when y'all get there."

"Sure will," I said as I hopped in the driver's side of Alex's car and pulled off toward home.

He talked almost the whole way there. Some of it I understood; some of it I missed because I was hoping and dreaming that tonight I would see what his dick felt like inside of me.

We pulled up to the building and I got out of the car and hurried around to the other side to help him out.

"Jazz, you are a lifesaver. I don't know I would do without you." His speech was slurred as he talked. But he had a smile on his face the whole time. I hoisted one of his arms around my shoulder as I helped him get out of the car. I made sure the door was locked and we walked up to the entrance of the building. I put my finger up to the fingerprint reader and the door unlocked so we could get in. We walked up the two flights of steps to where our homes were.

"We made it home," he said as he leaned up against the doorpost.

"Yes, we are home." I smiled. He put his finger on the fingerprint reader to his house and I helped him inside.

"I'm going to lay you in the bed and undress you and then go home," I said as I helped him down the hall to his bedroom. It was a mess. His bed wasn't made and clothes were everywhere. But that didn't deter me. As soon as we got over to the bed he fell backward as if he couldn't make it any farther. He was passed out cold. I almost let out a cackling type of laugh, but I held it in.

I kneeled down and took off his shoes and then his socks. I got up, leaned over, and unbuckled his belt. I pulled his pants off by the bottom of his pants until he was lying on his bed with his only his boxers and a shirt on. A wicked smile had covered my face. I was beyond ecstatic right now.

"Alex," I called out to him. He didn't answer. I said it a few more time a little bit louder. Still no response. So I walked around the bed to where his head was and slapped him lightly to see if he was really out of it. Still no response.

"All right, show time," I said as I crawled onto his bed and over to him. I hovered over him and marveled at the beautiful specimen that was before me. I pushed his shirt up and felt his upper body. It was magnificent.

"Yessssss. You're all mines now," I said as I rubbed him down. I leaned over and kissed his abdomen a few times. I was getting wet down below. I had on a dress so I lifted it up and over my head, freeing my breasts.

I then reached my hand over to his crotch area and smoothed my hands around. I then started to squeeze it and play with it. I was losing my mind. I then reached in and pulled him out of the slit in his boxers. My eyes widened at its girth.

"I've been waiting for you all of my life," I said as I started to massage it up and down. Alex groaned a bit and then shifted a little on the bed, causing me to pause in fear. It only lasted a second. I started breathing again and then I leaned over and took him in my mouth. He grew with every slurp that I took. I was taking it in my mouth as best I could, but he had a thick monster that filled my mouth up. I could only imagine what it was going to feel like to have him inside of me. A few more slurps and I couldn't wait any longer. I quickly straddled him and put his dick at the entrance of my womb. I eased down slowly and gasped halfway down his shaft. I covered my mouth as tears welled up in my eyes. It felt so good to be here right now. I eased down the rest of the way hoping that the pain that I was in right now would subside. I would have never imagined that he was packing like this. I began to slowly rock until I had a rhythm going. My juice began to flow and pretty soon I was pounding his lap getting all of the past years of frustration and horniness out of me. I came numerous times but that didn't matter right now. I was waiting for him to fill me up with his seed. I wanted to make this time worth it. I was in peak fertility right now and I wanted to be the mother of his children.

I rode him and rode him and rode him some more. It seemed like it was taking him forever to come. I knew that it was the liquor that he drank holding up the process, but I wasn't giving up until I got what I wanted. Twenty minutes later his body involuntarily jerked as I rode him letting me know that his little soldiers were shot up in me like a rocket leaving NASA.

I stayed put for a few moments to make sure that everything was good. When I was sure, I pulled myself off of him and it felt like my womb was relieved from all of the pressure it went through. I tucked his dick back in his boxers as best I could, kissed him on the cheek, and exited his house. As soon as I got into my apartment my phone chimed.

It was a text from Ashley asking me if we made it in. I replied, yes, was in the shower; and she answered with, cool. . . later. I smiled and then rubbed my stomach with hope that this was the beginning of Alex's first child growing inside of me. I showered and then crawled up into bed a delighted woman.

Chapter 16

Troy

Milk Carton Mischief

It was late at night and I was out doing some surveillance but it wasn't for the case I was working for the city of Baltimore. This was personal. Ashley was out with Jasmine at a club. My excuse for not going was that I had work to do on a case. She didn't argue or question me. She trusted what I said to her. Poor fool. I was surprised she was so gullible. I had really been playing the part of the adoring boyfriend so well lately. It was making me sick. Especially after that fiasco at the restaurant the other day. I wasn't surprised that she liked pussy. She could have liked fucking dogs in an alley as far as I was concerned. It was in her blood. All the more reason to cut her off. I was staying close to her and her siblings until the job was done.

I was now watching Diana Parks coming out of a different club all together. She was with a group of girls and one guy. I assumed that they all went to the same college together. They all looked to be in their early twenties or very late teens. There was a whole mess of them going in and out of the club. It made me wonder if her parents knew all about her whereabouts. I didn't care, because this would be her last night of partying if I had to say something about it.

Pretty soon the small group dispersed and a noticeably intoxicated Diana and the young man made their way toward a parked car. After he helped her in the car he damn near skipped around to the other side of the car and hopped in. It didn't take long before the light in the car came on, the engine started, and they pulled off. I pulled off with them hoping that they would be typical horny teens and find somewhere secluded to get busy. After watching them go through a drive-thru for a late-night snack, I started trailing them again. I was becoming impatient as I drove a car or two's length behind them. I let a car in front of me for good measure a few times. We were now on the east side of the city in a park not too far from where she went to college. It was a breeding ground for sin: dark, secluded, and a perfect place for two youngsters to fuck in peace. There wasn't anyone else around surprisingly.

I parked a ways from them. I watched them start fumbling around in the car like they were supposed to. I was dressed in all black from head to toe with gloves to match. I got myself ready to make my move. I had a lot of work to do in a little amount of time. I eased out of my car and snuck up on the passenger's side of the car. They had some music playing so they couldn't hear me anyway. I had a gun in one hand and a chloroform-soaked cloth in the other. Without warning I popped up and shot the boy in the head and covered her mouth with the cloth muffling a scream that may have caused some attention to be drawn to the area and me. There was no one around but you never knew who else was lurking about in the shadows.

I quickly opened the door to the car and scooped her now-limp body out and over my shoulder. I closed the door to the car and made my way back to the one I was driving. I popped open the trunk with the button on my key ring and laid her in the trunk. I quickly tied her hands and feet and placed a nice thick piece of duct tape around her mouth with a piece of cloth in her mouth to prevent her from chewing through the tape with her teeth.

I hopped back in the driver's side of my car and pulled away from the scene of the crime a happy camper. I had a long drive ahead of me.

I pulled up to my destination in record time. It was still dark outside. I didn't worry about anyone seeing though because I was a far cry from the city. It was a place I thought about all of the time. It was a part of my nightmare and my revenge. My life changed here. It ended here. A new me was birthed here. Theirs would end here.

I exited the car, popped the trunk, and threw the now–wide awake Diana over my shoulders. She squirmed and wiggled but I kept my pace toward our destination. I opened the door. The smell of memories flooded my nostrils. I stood in the middle of the living room and inhaled.

"Home." I smiled.

I lingered for only a moment as I made my way up the stairs and to the room where it was all going to happen, again. This time I would be the director. The cast was preset and I was writing the script. No happy ends for this one though.

I placed Diana in a chair that was in the room. I used some rope that I had to tie her down and made sure she was super secure. I didn't want her to escape and foil my plan.

"Hey, baby girl. I know your mind is racing right now as to why I am doing this and who I really am. We don't have time for introductions right now, but we will soon." I looked in her eyes as tears flowed from hers. I checked her pockets for her cell phone, Bluetooth, and any other electronic device. I pulled a metal detector wand out from under the bed and scanned her whole body for any type of transmitting device that may have been implanted on her body. Technology was something else. You could never be too careful. I took all of her jewelry off and everything that looked like it could be used to store something for tracking her.

Her pocketbook was left in the car where I first got her. I didn't care about that at all. I took her cell phone and Bluetooth so I could destroy them. No one would know she was here.

After I was sure she was secure I exited the house and made my way back to my home so I could get an hour or two of sleep.

I parked my car in my garage, changed the fake plates I had on it back to the ones that were registered to me and made my way into my home. I showered and lay down for about two hours before I hopped back up and left for a full day of work. Yes, I worked weekends too. My job was never done.

"Detective Crawford, we got another murder, this time at a club. I need you on the scene immediately. It's at a club called Wet. Get over there."

It didn't take long for me to spring into action. I was out of my office, in a vehicle, and headed over to the scene of the crime within minutes.

I pulled up to the scene about fifteen minutes later. The place was swarming with cops and various other people. I crossed under the yellow tape and made my way into the establishment. This was the place that Ashley said she went to last night.

A few people gave me nods as I walked back to where most of the activity going on. Someone handed me some gloves as soon as I entered the bathroom. Forensics was already on the scene but they cleared away for me as soon as I walked in.

"What's going on, fellas? Tell me something," I said as I looked at two officers who were standing nearby.

"The club's manager said they came in here before they closed the club to see if anybody was in here, but they only yelled to see if anyone was still in here and no one responded. The owner showed up this morning and she came in the bathroom to relieve herself and as a habit she checked the stalls. She noticed that the handicapped stall was locked and so she knocked a few times and got no response. She looked underneath and noticed a body on the toilet. That's when she called the police."

"Okay. I'm sure you have all of this documented already." I looked at both of them.

"Yes, sir," he answered.

"Make sure it's on my desk ASAP," I said and then turned to the lead forensic scientist. "Give me the breakdown?" I asked him.

"Well, this looks like a scene from a few of the other girls we have found. They all fit the same description. Young African American females, scantily dressed, weave, et cetera. It looks like her neck was broken but we will know more once we take her downtown."

"Fingerprints?" I asked.

"None, but we are still searching for more foreign fibers, hairs, or anything out of the ordinary. This is going to be hard, because this is a club and the atmosphere gets pretty congested in these types of arenas. We may find numerous fibers and hairs other than her own on her." He looked at me with a skeptical undertone to his words.

"I hear you but I'm going to need something. Work this scene over twice if you have to. I'm going to need everyone out of here who isn't forensics. This is a crime scene, not a sideshow," I barked. A few looked at me with side eyes but they followed the instruction. This had Alex all over this. I hoped that I was wrong. He was pissing me off by fucking with my plans.

***

It was a bright and sunny Sunday afternoon when I picked Ashley up for a trip downtown to the Baltimore National Aquarium. I was really growing tired of this boyfriend act.

"You are looking lovely today," I commented as we pulled into a parking spot in a parking garage near the aquarium.

"Thank you." She blushed.

We both exited the car and walked the few blocks to our destination. I had to admit I was having a great time at the aquarium. We took pictures and even held hands. After we had our fill of that we made our way to get something to eat at The Cheesecake Factory that was nearby.

After we were seated and our food was ordered, I decided that it was time for me to get the information that I needed to get out of her. This was a business and pleasure type of date.

"So did you have fun last night?" I asked as I gazed into her eyes. Her eyes sparkled with love. Too bad it was all a lie.

"Yes, I really enjoyed myself." She offered up a smile. "But I would have had even more fun if you were there with me."

"I'm sorry, baby. This case I'm working on is consuming my time. I hardly have any time to do anything personal." I lied on all counts. The lines between business and personal were beginning to blur in my world.

"It's okay, because I know that you have to do your job. I'm proud of your commitment to your job and to me."

"I do my best." I smiled proudly. "Was it you and Jasmine who went out last night?"

"At first it was only us, but we hooked up unexpectedly with my brother Alex and one of his groupies named Destiny at the club." She laughed.

"Oh, really," I said, happy that she gave me the information that I needed. "When is he going to settle down with one chick?" I laughed, but I was serious. I was hoping and praying that he had another good alibi.

"You know I was wondering the same thing myself. He's been off the hook ever since we moved back here from California. I'm going to have another talk with him about his choice in the girls he dates."

"Why doesn't he get together with Jasmine?" I asked. "She seems like a good girl."

"Nope," she said shaking her head. "Not going to happen."

"Why not?" I inquired.

"Alex won't date anyone I'm friends with, and since she's my best friend, she is totally off-limits."

"Too bad." I shook my head. "They probably would be a great couple."

"True." She nodded her head in agreement.

The waiter appeared back at our table as we finished talking. I was ecstatic on the inside. I now had to find out why Alex was using Jasmine as his alibi and if their relationship was real. I smelled some deception going on and it wasn't my own.

Chapter 17

Ashley

Lie to Me

I was sitting in my office finishing up making notes from a session I had with the city family I was working with to get to root of some of their problems. I wasn't a counselor per se. I was an in-between: a family's free resource before professional therapy. The problems that these people faced were no different from the families who lived in the suburban area. They dealt with them differently though. It made me think about my past and some of the things that my family made it through. Both families were making strides in their relationships with each other but there was still a ways to go. I was going to recommend each of the family members seek individual counseling as soon as they finished their time with me. Each family got recommended to this agency through social services and they were allotted ten sessions in a three-month period. I had a caseload of about five at the moment. Most were being recommended to go on to professional counseling services.

I was tired after this long day. All I wanted to do was get something to eat and make my way home. I had a great weekend, spending it with Jasmine on Saturday and then with Troy on Sunday.

Troy and I took a trip to the Baltimore National Aquarium. It was a great way to get to be with each other and have a good time. We walked hand-in-hand and even took a few pictures of each other.

"Wow." I shook my head in amazement as I gathered my things and made my exit from my office. I was never really the lovey-dovey type and here I was in a relationship and I was behaving myself.

I exited my office and said good-bye to a few other associates in the office and then left the building. I walked across the parking lot to my car with a smile on my face. As soon as I hopped in my car my phone began to ring. It was Jasmine.

"Hello," I answered with my Bluetooth.

"Hey, girl, what are you doing?" she asked. She sounded happier than normal.

"I just got off of work," I said as I started my car and then pulled out of my parking spot. "Why, what's up?"

"I have some news for you," she said with excitement.

"Girl, what?" I inquired with the same amount of excitement.

"I can't tell you over the phone. This is some face-to-face news."

"Okay, where we going to meet up at?" I asked.

"Meet me at our spot."

"Okay, I'll see you shortly," I said and then hung up the call.

It didn't take me long to get to where we were going to meet up. I parked my car and hopped out on a mission.

I walked through the doors of the Famous Dave's in Owings Mills when the memories of my past floated into my mind. I met but didn't meet the man who fathered me here in this restaurant so long ago. It was a very brief encounter, but I remembered it well. My mother and father said he was a real pistol. A bad boy to the core, but with a heart buried deep within. I encountered some of that same hotheadedness in some of my own endeavors. But look at me now. I had his blood in me, but it was only half of me. I was now tapping into the loving and passionate side about me.

"Hey, girl," Jasmine called out as she saw me coming in and made her way from over in the waiting area to the left. I looked at her in her scrubs and remembered how unstable she was in high school. She was as wild as I was. I guessed it was true that you attract those like you. Look at us now, both stable ladies in life.

"Hey, Jazz." I greeted her with a tight hug. We walked to the podium and were seated immediately. There weren't many people here because it was a Monday. I was waiting for her to spill the news. I was bubbling with curiosity. "So, girl, what is this news you have for me?" I looked at her intently. We were interrupted by the waitress popping up at the table. It didn't take me long to order what I wanted, because I always ordered the same thing. Jasmine, on the other hand, was taking a few minutes too long for me.

"Girl, hurry up so we can talk. The pigs in the back about to come back to life and get the hell out of here." I laughed trying to hurry her up. She took the push and ordered her meal.

As soon as the waitress walked away I looked at her and waited.

"Okay, so you ready?" she said in a teasing manner.

"Jasmine." I looked at her with a fake attitude.

"Okay." She smiled hard. "I'm pregnant."

"What!" I belted out louder than normal. I quickly covered my mouth, but it was too late. A few heads had already turned in our direction.

"I know right." She continued to smile. "I'm still shocked about it too."

"Shocked. Girl, I'm mystified." I looked at her with curiosity. "Who and when?"

"Well, I can't say anything about the 'who' because I haven't told him yet. And we have been involved with each other for a while now. We have been getting very close over time and, well, now we are closer than ever."

"Damn, Jazz, you've been holding out on me." I smiled even though I was slightly disappointed that she kept this from me. It was her life so I had to respect her and her choices.

"I know. I was dying to tell you but I had to hold out until I was sure." She gave me an apologetic look.

"Girl, it's all right. I'm so excited for you." I felt a tear threatening to fall. I quickly wiped it away. These tears and vulnerability were getting the best of me.

"I'm so happy that you are happy for me." She started crying too. I couldn't believe that we were two crying fools here in the middle of this restaurant.

"Jazz, are you going to go and tell your mom about this?" I inquired.

The look on her face was of pure shock. You would have thought I had said a bad word or something.

"I don't know." She looked away from me for a moment. Her mother had a lot of mental instability. She had taken her husband's life right after we graduated from high school. Jasmine was a daddy's girl. I knew it rocked her world, but she rarely talked about it. I couldn't remember a time that I saw her cry about it. But maybe she was a private person with her emotions. "She might not even know who the hell I am." She frowned up her face.

"Jazz, I think it would be a good chance to go see her. Maybe she would understand." I tried my best to sound optimistic. Truth was, I was told that her mother was heavily medicated and most of the time she was in a drone-like state. At least that was what Jasmine told me.

"I don't know." She shook her head. "It will be something that I have to think about."

"I understand." I nodded my head in agreement. "I can go with you if that will make you feel better?"

"Well, if I do decide to go then I will need someone to go with me." She smiled. I was glad that she was even thinking about it.

Our food was delivered moments later. We ate and laughed and went over possible baby names for the baby growing in her belly.

Afterward we hugged and went our separate ways.

I hopped in my car and began my journey home. My phone began to ring and I answered, "Hello."

"Ash, I need you to stop by the house as soon as possible. It's important," my mother requested and then hung up in my ear. Her tone wasn't normal, so I pushed the pedal to the metal and got going.

Chapter 18

Alex

Backup

I walked into my office this fine Monday morning still a little drained from Saturday night. I didn't even leave the house on Sunday. I was completely out of it. I couldn't recall anything that happened after Jasmine told me that she saw my girl—and I used that term loosely because apparently she was loose—go into the men's bathroom with another guy. I couldn't say I was really shocked but that was a down low and dirty move, since she had given me some head before we left my house. I mean really talk about a busy broad. She definitely got the slob that knob VIP award.

Anyway, a brother still was dragging. You would have thought that I got some ass that night, too. I mean I woke up in my boxers on and my pants on the floor. I was baffled at the fact that I had some dried-up cum on my boxers and the inside of my thigh and my dick was as well. I remembered Jasmine helping me in the house and into my bedroom. I vaguely remembered her telling me she was going to undress me and leave, but after that it was all a blank for me.

"I have to stop drinking like that. I could've been fucked by a dude and never even knew about it." I shook my head in disappointment.

It wasn't long before I started my day and got some work done. I had to go over some contracts and get some calls in so I got a few clients some endorsements. I wanted to upgrade my car and possibly my living situation. I wasn't strapped for money but I wanted to have a little more than I had at the moment. The more money they made the more I made and the agency as well.

A few hours later there was a knock on my door. "Come in," I called out.

Lance came into my office with an even more sorrowful look than the last time he was in my office. He looked like he was at death's door. I'd never seen him look so worn for wear. His clothes were mismatched and he had a nappy head. This brother surely didn't know how to hide his problems.

"How's it going?" I smiled as I reached my hand across my desk to shake his as he sat down. I knew the situation, but I didn't want to add to his misery by going right in on it.

"Man, I might as well pack my shit up now and get on the next train to my momma's house. This dude is going for the jugular with this extortion business. He wants three million dollars from me to keep quiet and he's giving me three weeks to come up with it."

I was speechless for a few moments. I was in the wrong business. I needed to be blackmailing a few folks to get ahead in this rat race called life. $3 million would set a brother up real nice right about now. I smiled unknowingly.

"Yo, Alex, what you smile for?" he asked with a confused look on his face. "This some real shit I'm in right now. I'm about to be ass out in a few. I need a solution to this mess. You talk to your father?" He scooted up in his chair and put both of his hands on the desk, waiting for an answer from me.

"I'm sorry about that. I was thinking about this weekend," I lied. "I have not talked to my father about this yet, because I had another plan."

"And what plan was that?" He looked at me with hope in his eyes.

"Well, I was going to call in a friend for a favor, but I can't tell you anything about it. I want you to be knowledge-free if it should go awry."

"So what am I supposed to do while you working this out?"

"I need you to go home, take a bath." I looked at him and frowned, hinting at his present appearance. "And I need you to act as normal as you possibly can. You can't let people see you frazzled, like the way you are looking right now."

"I know, man." He looked ashamed. "I didn't know how to deal with this. I mean my wife is asking questions about why I am so quiet and the slightest noise rattles me. I mean, man, this is some serious shit. I am leaving this sex-crazy shit alone."

"I truly hope so, because when you get out of this it will be a memory and feeling that should make you keep yourself in the house for good."

"True that." He nodded his head.

"Listen, I need you to forward me all of the texts and videos that dude sent you so I can get someone to analyze it for me. We are going to get you out of this mess for sure." I smiled as hard as I could, hoping that he would retain some of the positive vibes I was sending his way.

"Well, I have to get busy on this and I need you to get busy on your part. I will call you with updates," I said getting up and walking around my desk. I shook his hand and pulled him in for a slight embrace. It was to reassure him that I was on his side. I did have a hint of a plan in the back of my own mind on how to get paid out of this situation as well. I mean this was a service I was doing for him on the side. Why not get paid on the side as well?

I let fifteen minutes go by before I reached for my phone and dialed the number I was looking for. It was an old friend and I had not spoken to him in a few so right now was as good a time as ever.

The phone rang a few times before he picked up.

"Wassup, Wallace." I leaned back in my chair. I smiled because the memories of the times we had in California flooded back into my mind. Some were good and some were not so good. But we made it through it all. We all were the better for all that we went through. "Long time no hear." I laughed.

"Hey, wassup, Lex. How's it going back there in Baltimore? You and Ashley staying out of trouble?" He laughed a little.

"Man, I can say that life is problem free right now," I boasted.

"That's good to hear. How are your parents and the rest of the crew?" he inquired.

"Wallace, they are all doing great. Everyone is doing wonderful."

"So to what do I owe the pleasure of this call?"

I laughed before I answered, "I see you are still right to the point with things."

"Well, it was the tone of your voice that gave you away."

"Really?" I wondered.

"Yep."

"Okay, here's the problem. One of my clients ran into a problem and I need to get your assistance on it."

"Cool, what you need?" he asked. I loved the fact that he didn't interrogate me on the ins and outs of the matter. That was a friend for you.

"Well, I don't have all the details yet, but as soon as I do I will get back up with you. I was calling you to give you a heads-up."

"Great. I will be ready to help as best I can when I get the call. I have to take care of some business with the restaurant so I have to get off of this phone. Love you, young soldier. Until next time."

"Until next time," I said as I hung up the phone.

As weird as our relationship was in the beginning, you know, finding out about him and my biological father being lovers and the rest of the mess that we went through because of it, I was amazed that it all worked out and we remained friends to this day. He was actually one of my closest friends even though he lived clear across the country. He was only a phone call away. It was nice to have true friendship.

I made some more business calls and then sent the videos and text messages to a friend of mine to get them analyzed and then went to lunch.

My day went pretty smooth after lunch and now I was headed out of my office when my telephone began to vibrate. It was my father.

"Son, I need you home ASAP. I'll explain when you get here." He hung up abruptly. I tried not to wonder but I was baffled as I left my office, hopped in my car, and made my way to my parents' house.

Chapter 19

Jasmine

Pregnant Possibilities

"Hi, how are you?" A warm smile covered the face of a Motherhood Maternity store employee as I walked in with a smile that easily challenged hers. I had taken half the day off so I could beat the regular mall traffic at Arundel Mills Mall in Hanover, Maryland. "What can I help you with today?"

"I found out that my husband and I are expecting our first child or children, I hope." I looked around the store like a kid in a candy shop. Tears welled up in my eyes.

"Are you okay?" She came from behind the counter and walked over to me. She started to rub my back. The tears really began to flow then. I was hunched over a bit. She then cradled me in her arms.

I sobbed and sobbed and then lifted my head. "We have been trying for so, so long. I . . . I didn't think it was going to happen you know." I looked at her and a smile began to resurface on my face.

"I'm so glad that you are expecting." She continued to rub my back. It was a motherly type of rub, too. It made me think of my mother and her drama. I cringed at the thought.

"I'm okay now," I snapped and then walked away. She looked at me, and confusion covered her face. "So what do you have for beginning mothers?"

"How far along are you?" she asked as her smile resurfaced on her face as well.

"About a week," I lied and smiled proudly. It had only been two full days since I let Alex explode his seed into my womb.

"Oh." She looked at me strangely.

"What's wrong?" I asked.

"Nothing, it's . . ." Her voice trailed off and then she walked away. I followed.

"It's what?" She was in a corner of the store as I approached her. She was pretending to be folding some clothes but I didn't care. "What were you going to say?" I moved in closer to her. My voice was filled with attitude and curiosity. I wanted to know what she was going to say. I demanded it actually.

"I . . . I wasn't going to say anything," she nervously fumbled, looking past me in hopes of a rescue. It was only she and I in the store.

"Bitch, say it," I growled as I leaned into her direction. I was damn near kissing her.

"I was going to say isn't it a little early for maternity shopping?" She spoke in a low tone. She was afraid. She was a thin black woman, probably in her thirties. I wasn't huge but I could easily take her. She knew it.

"What does that mean?" I huffed. "You are all up in my business. You are supposed to be a saleswoman. Now sell me something before I lose it and beat your ass in here. If I wanted counsel I would have asked for it. Acting like you are a walking pregnancy test and shit," I said as I backed up off of her. She looked a little relieved as I moved out of her vicinity and browsed through a few racks. She made her way back toward the register area. I watched her out of the corner of my eyes, in case she was calling security or something.

I picked out a few pieces of clothing, mainly T-shirts with catchy phrases like "Eating for two," "Bun in the oven," and a few others. I walked up to the register with my selections and put them on the counter.

"Will that be all?" she asked as she hurriedly rang my things up and stuffed them in the bag.

I looked at her with an evil glare. "I think you might want handle my shit with a little more care. Tossing my clothes in the bag won't get me out of here faster, but it will get you tossed up in here faster. Fold my shit right," I said looking her dead in the eyes. Today wasn't the day to try me.

She did as she was told and took each piece out and folded it like it was supposed to be folded. I handed her my credit card and she processed my payment and handed me my card back. She didn't even look at me while she did it. I knew her ass wanted me out of the store but I was leaving when I wanted to not hastily like she was trying to make me leave.

She handed me my purchase and turned to do something behind her. "What? No 'Have a nice day?'"

"Have a nice day," she said over her shoulder. It took everything in me not to snatch her but I didn't want to risk hurting the baby growing inside of me.

I walked around the mall for a little bit, grabbed myself something to eat, and caught a movie. As soon as I exited the movie theater my phone began to ring. I fumbled through my purse to find it and when I did I immediately pressed ANSWER.

"Hey, girlie, wassup?" I greeted Ashley.

"Girl, it's some serious stuff going down. Can you come over to my parents' house ASAP?" she asked.

"Sure, Ash. I'm on my way. What's wrong?" I asked with concern.

"I can't explain right now. I need you here."

"All right, see you shortly." I hung up the phone, threw it back in my purse, and left the mall. It didn't take me long to get to my car because I was walking at a quick pace. Ashley sounded stressed. I had to go and see what was going on.

Chapter 20

Troy

Good stuff

Blood was everywhere.
The piercing screams that I could still hear.
The revenge in his voice.
The pleading in hers.
The fear that filled my body as I stood there helpless and paralyzed.
What could I do?
I was a child.
What could I do?
I lay naked in my bed, sweat covering my body. I was deep in the past. This was an occurrence that happened a few times a week since that day. It left me weak and drained. The thoughts of that night drained my life. But I rolled over, sat up, and placed my feet firmly onto my wood floor. I stood up and stretched my body. I walked over to the full-length mirror that was on the back of my door and admired my body. I was in shape. I had an exercise regimen that kept me fit. I had an athlete's body.

It was four o'clock in the morning: the time I got up daily. I turned back around and walked back toward my bed. I immediately removed the damp linen. I placed it in the hamper on the other side of the room and quickly made a trip to my linen closest for a replacement. After I was finished with that I made my way out of my room and toward my in-home gym. I spent a half hour in this room this morning before making my way to the bathroom to shower, shave, and brush my teeth. I dressed and made my way toward my basement. I lived in a ranch-type house that was perfect for me.

My basement consisted of three rooms: a recreation room, bathroom, and my task force room. I headed right toward my task force room. In it was my whole life's work. It was padlocked for my protection. I unlocked it and opened the door. I inhaled as I entered the room. It was my sanctuary. I had all my research posted up on all of the walls. I had social site pictures up of Ashley, Alex, Diana, and their father, James Parks. Autopsy documents, birth certificates, obituaries, and more. Being a police officer I had access to many things. I had phone records. I had so much on them. They were going down. I spent about fifteen minutes in the room before I made my way back up to the kitchen for a quick breakfast.

I quickly fixed a bowl of oatmeal, wheat toast, and a glass of orange juice. I cleaned up my dishes and made my way out of my house. I drove my regular route to work, which only took me about thirty minutes.

I walked into the precinct with a lot on my mind, mainly the case of these murdered girls. The new one that I was waiting for the results on was at the forefront of my mind the most. I couldn't get it out of my mind. This one was a little different from the other girls. It looked desperate and unplanned. If this was the same person doing these killings, they were definitely getting sloppy.

I walked into my office and promptly turned my laptop on. There was a knock on the door that unnerved me instantly. I hated to be disturbed most of the time, but mornings were the most irritating to me. I didn't like to be disturbed before I prepped myself for work. The first few minutes of my workday in the office were dedicated to reading over my notes from the day before. Now here someone was interrupting the flow.

"Come in," I yelled. Irritation was mixed in on purpose. My so-called partner walked in through the door.

"Hey, good morning." The officer who helped me interrogate Alex the first time came in with a jubilant smile on his face. Not only did he play the good cop in our times together in the interrogation room, he was a happy person all of the time. Now I didn't hate that. I wasn't feeling it this early in the morning. The pressure was on about this case and I was trying to prove myself and handle my personal life as well. I was focused and happy didn't fit at the moment.

"Good morning," I spoke low and with little enthusiasm. "What can I help you with?"

"Wow, dude, what got your goat this morning?" He looked at me with the same smile.

My countenance didn't change either. I wanted to be alone. "Nelson, what can I do for you?" I looked at him straight in the eye. It was one of the first times I actually did. He was different. I rose from my seat, walked around my desk, closed my door, and made sure it was locked. I was glad that this moment had happened. I had been pent up for so long. I needed a release. I needed one bad.

"I was here to check in on you with the case. Since we are supposed to be working together." He was still facing my desk as he talked. I walked up behind him.

"Nelson, there is something about you. Something different." I put my hand on his shoulder as I stood in close proximity to him. I felt his uneasiness as his shoulders tensed up.

"Wh . . . why you say that?" He turned his head toward me as his voice quivered out the words he spoke.

"Well, I have heard some disturbing things about you and paid them no mind most of the time, but today I am very interested in seeing if they are true."

"Wh . . . what have you heard?" His voice continued to resound in nervousness.

I unlatched my belt, with one hand still on his shoulder, unzipped my pants, reached in for my already-rock hard manhood and pulled it out.

"I heard that the warm of your mouth is divine." I walked around the side of him so he could get a good view at my throbbing piece of meat.

The look on his face and the gulp of his hard swallow let me know that the rumor was true. He was a meat eater. Truth was I didn't hear anything about him around here because I stayed to myself but as the saying goes, "It takes one to know one." I knew he was one. He was a good-looking one, too. I was able to control myself most of the time but today my flesh was calling the shots and this opportunity presented itself. I was answering the call.

"What do you want me to do with that?" He suddenly turned back around and faced my desk as if I was lying and the saliva that had involuntarily slid out of the side of his mouth didn't give him away.

"I want you to take your time and put it in your mouth. We both know you want it," I said as I took it and waved it from side to side with my hips. He looked out of the side of his eye.

"You have me mixed up with someone else." He hopped up out the chair and made his way toward the door.

"No, you are him. Come and get it. I know you want this load in your mouth and oozing slowly down your throat. You know it." I walked up on him and put my hand on his shoulder once again. This time he was face to face with me. He was looking down toward the floor, at my dick most likely. I placed my other hand on his other shoulder and applied light pressure. He buckled and on his knees he went.

He took all of me in his mouth. The feeling that went through me was euphoric and pleasurable. My head fell backward as I palmed his curly haired head.

"Yes, suck it!" I moaned very low and sensuous. It had been a long and laboring time since I felt a mouth this good or at all for that matter. He took slow, long strides up and down my dick. I was glad that he was taking his time. He knew what he was doing. He never gagged or seemed stressed as I plunged the back of his throat a few good times in between his slow pace.

"You feel so good. You are doing well." I spoke low as his eyes looked up at me as most meat eaters did when they asked how they were doing with their eyes. He continued to wet my dick with his mouth like I liked it. But today I wanted more. I wanted to fuck. Fuck out some of my frustrations.

I reached down and pulled him up by one of his armpits. He had a look of disappointment on his face. No words needed to be spoken as I reached around him and palmed his firm behind. I pointed to the plush and sturdy chair that sat on the left side of my office wall. He walked over to it and then reached in his back pocket and pulled out his wallet. He pulled out a condom, which I figured his tramp ass would have, and placed it on the side arm of the chair. He pulled down his pants and positioned himself with his knees in the chair and hands holding the back of the chair.

I smiled as I walked up behind him, because it had been a long time since I fucked a dude or had one fuck me. I was on a self-imposed sexual hiatus until now. I remembered how it felt and I was looking forward to working out a good nut. I had to be careful not to make too much noise because I didn't want to attract any unwanted attention but I didn't want to take too long with fucking him. I had other things to do.

I placed the condom on my dick and proceeded to push myself inside of him. An "ahhh" escaped my mouth as my pelvis reached his butt. He didn't whimper or moan, he wiggled his behind in pleasure. I slowly ground into him for the first few thrusts, but it didn't take long for me to work up a good pace without slamming into him and making noise. He was good at being quiet as well. He took the dick well. I wasn't long in length but wide in girth. I had fucked a few dudes in the past who had no problems being vocal. In the back of my mind I was thinking that I would want to fuck Nelson again. Simply because of his obedience and cautiousness.

It didn't take long for me to cum in the condom and pull myself out. It was a great release and relief for me.

I walked over to my desk with my dick still out and opened the drawer to my desk that had some Wet Ones inside. I pulled out a few for myself before I took the container out and tossed it his way. I cleaned myself off as he did the same. He had a smile on his face. My facial expression changed back to the one I had on earlier. I sat down at my desk and began to get some work done. There was no more discussion needed between us. What else could be said? He got his need and want met and so did I. He exited the office and I smiled after he shut my door.

"Damn, that was some good ass," I said and then laughed. I reached down and massaged my hard-on that arrived back so quickly. I ignored it for the rest of the day.

After I left work, I made a short stop past the hospice to see Ma Dear and then went to check on Diana. I fed her, and bathed her almost every other day. Kidnapping was a task in itself. But my plans were coming together. I was glad about that.

Chapter 21

Ashley

Front Page News

I pulled up to the house that I grew up in and evolved in. I placed the car in park, turned the ignition off, and then secured the emergency brake. I looked in the mirror. I liked what I saw. I was a big girl now. My past was behind me and I was looking forward to my future, my destiny. I was so glad that Antoinette had spilled the beans about my past with women. She actually did me a favor. I didn't like the way that it was done, but hey, it was over now and I couldn't knock that. Now Troy and I could officially move forward.

"Let me get in this house." I opened the door of my car and stepped out. I parked in front of the house instead of the driveway, because that was filled with four cars already: one was my parents', one was Alex's, my grandmother's on my father's side, and I didn't recognize the fourth one. I walked around the front of my car and up to the waist-high wooden fence that encased part of my parents' front yard. Even this front yard had memories. I found one of my father's pair of underwear in the bushes underneath her and my father's bedroom-window after school and gave them to her. I was only five, but I knew that something was wrong with my father's underwear being in the bushes. I inquired to my mother about it after I handed them to her but I never got the answer to it because she dismissed me quickly with, "Young lady, your homework is waiting on you."

I laughed to myself as I placed my key in the front door and made my way inside of the house. There was no place like home.

I heard talking in the living room and made my way toward there. It was only a few steps from the door so it didn't take me long to get there.

"Good evening, everyone." I was concerned but not overly so until my I saw my mother, Brittany, and grandmother dabbing the corners of their eyes with tissue. The first thing I thought was that somebody had died. Fear instantly set in as I made my way across the room and next to Alex. I noticed pictures of my sister, Diana, spread out across the coffee table. That made me extremely curious.

"What's going on?" I asked no one in particular. My father had his head down and I couldn't see his face, but I knew that something was deeply wrong because he rarely got emotional out in the open.

"When was the last time you saw or spoke to Diana?" My father's head popped up out of nowhere.

"I . . . I, um . . ." I stammered as I quickly racked my brain trying to recall the last time I spoke to, texted, or saw her. I drew a blank. "I don't remember." It was amazing how much attention and detail we didn't pay to the ones close to us. Times like these showed that the proof was in the pudding. Everyone was about themselves most of the time. I couldn't even remember the last thing she had on or the last time that I told her that I loved her.

"What is going on?" I said with a little more agitation in my voice. I hated evasiveness. Get to the point and spit it out.

"They . . . they found your sister's car and boyfriend dead on the inside of the car," my grandmother said as she consoled my mother. "Your sister is nowhere to be found." My mother let out a sob as she lay over into my grandmother's arms and cried freely.

I felt her pain. Tears started to form at the corners of my eyes as well. The thought of my sister being missing and possibly dead was a bit overwhelming to think about it.

"Do they know how long she's been missing?" I, again, threw the question out there to no one in particular.

"We would have to say a day or two," a very dark-skinned guy said. He was in the room the whole time, but I truly didn't pay him any mind until now.

"Who are you?" I said with a little more attitude than what was called for. He caught me off guard. Normally my parents would have introduced him but under the present circumstances they weren't in the meet-and-greet mood. Understandably so.

"I'm Detective Holmes. I was assigned to the case this morning. We found the car Sunday night. It appeared to have been cold for twenty-four to thirty-six hours when it was discovered by a patrolling police vehicle. It was found in a highly unpopulated and popular hiding spot for illegal activities. Do you know if your sister was involved in any unusual behavior; drugs, prostitution, you know things like that?"

"What!" I immediately got offended. My voice escalated causing everyone to look at me. I felt my pressure rising and the old Ashley resurfacing. "Did you call my sister a drugging whore?"

"Ashley!" my mother said as she looked at me in shock. "Calm down. That's not what he said. You are overreacting. Let him finish."

"I'm sorry, but that is what it sounded like to me." I sat back in the chair, crossed my legs, folded my arms against my chest, and zipped my lips closed. I kept my eyes on the detective the whole time though. I knew what I heard.

"So does anyone in this room have any correspondence with Diana that can determine her last whereabouts before she became missing? Texts, voicemail, e-mail; anything will do."

"Well, she did tell me that she was going to the club when I talked to her on Saturday." My little sister Brittany spoke. She was a quiet girl. The quietest of the family you might say. She was very patient and always even tempered. Everyone looked at her as she spoke.

"Did she happen to tell you what club it was she was going to?" the detective asked, with notepad in hand, ready to take notes.

"No, she didn't say." Brittany looked disappointed as she spoke.

"Okay," the detective said as he nodded his head and then proceeded to write on his pad.

"Have y'all found her cell phone?" Alex asked. I sat up in curiosity of the answer.

"The phone has yet to be recovered. In events of foul play, it is likely that the device has been destroyed. But we can still retrieve pertinent information through the person's cell phone coverage provider. I have her number and I called it in as soon as I found it in the phone of the deceased in the car. I am waiting for a subpoena to come back so that we can review records of her texts and hopefully voicemails."

"Why is this happening to us?" My mother burst out into a loud cry.

It hurt my heart to see her like this. Our family had been through a considerable amount of obstacles and this was not a needed or wanted addition to our memories.

Chapter 22

Alex

What's Going On?

Damn! My mother is wilding out, I thought as I looked at my mother in awe. I had never really witnessed my mother get this emotional. I mean I had observed her in an emotional state before, but not to this degree. You would have thought that we had the funeral and she was staring down at my sister's cold corpse. Now don't get it twisted, I was highly concerned about my sisters whereabouts too.

I then looked at my twin sister Ashley, who looked like she was about to blow a gasket any minute. I hadn't seen her this mad in a minute.

"Ash. Ash." I patted her on her leg to get her attention. She was somewhere else.

"What?" she asked and turned her head quickly in my direction.

"You okay?" I asked as I leaned back a little. Her chest was heaving up and down. I didn't know what to expect from any one of the women in my family. My grand-mother and Brittany were the calmest ladies in the room.

"Yeah, I'm a little agitated. This guy is asking for it." She turned to look at him and then back at me. He looked like he was ready to go.

There was a lot of emotion in the room. Even my father was a little distraught at the moment. It had me wondering what was going on. I couldn't fathom someone snatching and killing my little sister. You saw this in the news all the time but you never ever thought that it could happen to someone in your family and you never knew how to respond to such a shocking and devastating event.

"So what can we expect to happen in the next couple of hours or days?" I asked the detective.

"Frankly, this is too early in the case to tell. We have to interview her friends, college roommates, professors, and anyone in contact with her recently. Time is of the essence and from the looks of it we are two days behind."

My mother moaned loudly again and everyone turned their attention toward her for a moment.

"What are the odds of finding my daughter alive?" my father asked, turning the attention back toward the detective. He had the look of a desperate father on his face. One that was hoping to get a good response. A glimmer of hope. I had to say that I was anticipating the same.

"Mr. Black, right now it is fifty-fifty. The rest of this week I will be very busy handling interviews and calls. There is plenty of investigating to do. This has been a busy season for us down at the precinct. Young ladies being murdered is on the rise."

That information made my mother yelp again. My father lowered his head again.

"Sir, that is information you could have kept to yourself," Ashley said with a mean mug on her face. "How in the hell is that helping the situation right now?"

"Ash, calm down. It's all right. He is giving it to us straight," I said as I tried to calm her down by rubbing her back. It didn't help that the detective had a red shirt on because Ashley was like a bull seeing red right now. She was ready to charge right now.

"Well, lie to me then next time, mutha—" she said and then I quickly covered her mouth before the rest could get out.

"Ash, let's go get some water for Mom." I quickly got up and pulled her right along with me until we were in the kitchen.

"Did you hear him in there? He was so insensitive. How was he gonna be talking about murdered girls and shit? Miss me with that shit," she said as she pulled out a chair and sat down at the table.

I walked to the refrigerator and pulled out two bottles of water. I sat down across from her and then slid a bottle of water her way. She really needed to cool down. She was cursing like a sailor and it wasn't like her as of late to be doing such. I needed her to calm down before we went back into the other room. Mom and Dad didn't need any added tension in the room.

"Ash, he was being honest. I heard about some of what he was saying recently." The thought of the three chicks being murdered and me being in the precinct a few days earlier flashed through my mind. It was not the best image I needed right now.

"Honest," she said and then she huffed in frustration. "His ass was being morbid. There's no hope; that is what he was saying on the sly." She banged on the table and startled me in the process.

"Ashley, that is not true. There is hope. We are going to find Diana alive and well. We will, I promise." I reached over and grabbed her by the hand.

"You think so?" She looked at me in the eyes. A few tears fell down her face as she stared at me. The anger was a front for the pain that she was feeling. She was trying to be tough as usual but she was holding up the front as good as she thought she could.

"Yes, we have God and faith. That is all we need," I said sincerely.

"She's alive. I can feel it," she said as she perked up a bit. A small smile came across her face.

"I know she is too," I said as I smiled too. Our family had been through some great stumbling blocks and made it through. This too would pass. "Besides she has some James Parks in her, too." I laughed lightly. She did as well.

"Yeah, we are survivors." She nodded her head.

"Are you ready to go back in there?" I asked her.

"Yes."

"Are you going to behave?" I said teasing her.

"I promise." She put her hand over heart. "Cross my heart and hope to die." She laughed lightly again.

"Okay, let's get back in there," I said as I got up from the table and waited for her to do the same. We walked back to the other room but before we both could sit back down the doorbell rang.

"I'll get it," I said as I exited the room and made my way to the front door.

Chapter 23

Jasmine

Baby, Baby, Baby

I stood at the door and waited for someone to answer. I was curious as to what was going on because there were so many cars parked in the driveway. I had my shopping bags in hand. Mainly, my Motherhood Maternity bag. I wanted to gush about the fact that I was expecting. I couldn't wait until Mrs. Black found out about the baby, which would be her first grandchild. I knew she was going to be excited as I was. I was finally going to have a mother and a father again. All I had to do was murder a couple of chicks and, voila, I was pregnant and about to have some in-laws. Life was grand.

The front door popped open and my baby daddy was standing there with all of his finesse oozing out of his pores. He had on a nice shirt and tie set that made him look so dashing. Damn, I was a lucky girl. Shit, looking at him for these brief seconds I could still feel his dick like he was inside of me right now. I wanted to ride him again. I had to. I was waiting for the next opportunity to do so.

"Hey, Jazz," he greeted me. He looked a little down in the face.

"Hey, baby dad . . . boy. Baby boy," I said catching my slip-up for the like the millionth time. I was going to have to get my shit together before he thought I was crazy or something. "How is everything?"

"Okay, but it could be better," he said as he stepped back and let me in the house. "Everybody is in the living room."

"Okay." I smiled at him as I took my jacket off and handed it to him. He looked at my ass on the sly. I smiled at him letting him know that I had seen him. Then I made my way into the living room.

As soon as I got there, there was a depressed-looking crowd who filled the seats of the nice furniture. It made me even more curious. I walked over and sat next to Ashley with my interest bubbling.

"Girl, you okay? I came as soon as I could." I looked at her with concern and then looked around the room again really quickly. There was a suit-and-tie type of guy sitting across the room. He had a serious look on his face.

"Jazz, my sister Diana is missing. She been missing since Saturday."

"Really? Oh my goodness. I'm so sorry to hear that. I can't believe that." Concern filled my voice. I couldn't imagine have a missing family member. With all the things going on right now in this city, I knew they were thinking the worst. Who wouldn't?

"Yes, girl. We all are shook right now. The detective over there is in charge of the case. We are praying and hoping for the best possible turnout. We have hope." She smiled. It was a light one. One that was filled with optimism and some doubt. A natural response to this type of situation.

"Yes, girl. She probably ran off or something. These young girls are something else. She's probably snuggled up with her boyfriend somewhere." I tried to sound reassuring.

"He's dead. They found him dead in his car," she said with as her eyes began to water up.

"Really?" I covered my mouth is shock. That wasn't a good piece of information to know. He was dead and her sister was missing. That sounded like an open-and-shut case of murder and kidnapping or, worse, murder/murder. "Oh no."

"Yes, girl. That was my first response too." She shook her head. I looked around the room once again and it was still kind of quiet. Ashley and I had been talking in a hushed tone the whole time, trying not to disturb anyone or the situation.

"Mr. and Mrs. Black, I don't want to take up anymore of your time. I have to get back to the station and work the case. Time is of the essence. If you hear of anything please feel free to contact me," the detective said as he rose from his chair and walked over to where they were. He shook Mr. Black's hand and then turned to make his way to the door. Mr. Black followed him.

"Mona, let's get you upstairs and into bed for a few. I am staying over to help you with the house and the kids," Ashley's grandmother said as she helped Mrs. Black up from the chair and across the room. Mrs. Black was a strong woman but right now she was a blubbering mess. She didn't fight nor did she argue. She sobbed and walked toward the steps. They both disappeared up the steps out of sight. It made me feel some type of way to be in the house with such a sad scene going on.

"Girl, you want to see the shirts I got from Motherhood Maternity?" I perked up and asked Ashley.

"You went shopping already?" she asked. She seemed shocked by the gesture. I almost went off on her like I did the chick at the store earlier but I didn't. I held my tongue and thought before I spoke.

"Yeah, girl. No time like the present." I was almost bouncing in the chair.

"You pregnant?" Alex startled me as he came back into the room. He had a sandwich on a plate. It looked good.

"Yes." I beamed brightly. I was like a Mrs. Sunshine right now.

He looked at me strangely before he went and sat down on a chair near where we were sitting.

"Something wrong, Alex?" I asked him.

"Well . . ." He paused. "Oh, never mind." He waved his hand. "It's nothing."

"Go ahead and say it. You surprised, right?" I looked at him confirming the look he gave me.

"Well, uh. Yeah. I never really saw you with anyone. You know, a guy."

I was a little pissed at the statement but I let it slide because he was right. I really wanted to tell him he was the daddy, but that would be out of line at the moment for me. Besides his younger sister and brother, Brittany and Li'l Shawn, was in the room, but she was on some type of game thingy and he was on his phone. They were paying us no mind whatsoever. It was hush-hush news at the moment.

"I keep my business pretty private, Alex, if you must know. But yeah, I have a bun in the oven and the baby daddy and I are happy with our soon-to-be bundle of joy." I rubbed my stomach and smiled.

"Well, that is good to hear. I am happy for you." He smiled and then he pulled half of his sandwich off of his plate and took a bit. He moaned in satisfaction.

"Alex, you have a good-looking sandwich going on over there."

"Yes, it is good." He smiled. "You want a piece?"

"Sure, why not." I got up and made my way over to where he was. I picked up the other half of the sandwich and made my way back to my seat.

Ashley looked at me and then smiled. "Girl, you are really extra with the baby stuff."

"Shoot, I'm hungry. I'm eating for two you know." I laughed.

"Yes, that is true. But you better watch your figure because you may be eating for two but end up wearing clothes for three. Slow your roll, chick. You got plenty of time for all of that. Right now I need you to help me do some digging to find my sister. I can't leave her fate in the hands of some bumbling cops."

"Girl, I got you. I'm going wherever you are." I spoke earnestly.

"Glad to hear that because we have a lot of work to do."

"What work are you going to be doing?" Mr. Black asked as he entered the room again. He was a fine man himself and if his wife wasn't the feisty one I heard about I would have tried to get a baby out of him first. He has some good genes; then again he wasn't really their father but looking at Li'l Shawn I could tell he had some strong genes.

"Oh nothing, Dad. I was going to do some investigating myself." Ashley looked at her father with a little fear on her face. He didn't have a nasty look on his face but one of total seriousness.

"I need you kids to stay out of this. Let the police do their job. I don't want y'all messing this up. Promise me that you will stay out of this." He looked at all of us in the face. He made me nervous.

"Yes, sir," we all said in unison.

"Good, because I want my daughter back here safe and sound. I don't want anything happening to any of you in the process. We have enough to deal with now. I'm going upstairs to check on your mother. Lock up before you all leave. Li'l Shawn, I need you to take out the trash; and, Britt, load up the dishwasher for me."

They both followed the instructions that were given while Ashley, Alex, and I sat in the living room in silence.

The look on Ashley's face said that she said okay to him, but she was still going to do things her way anyway. She was headstrong and talking to her sometimes was like talking to a brick. I thought her father knew that as well because he came back into the room once more.

"I mean it, Ashley. Stay out of it." He looked at her intently.

"I will," she assured him.

As soon as he left the room she said, "Meet me tomorrow so I can go over a plan with Troy in the room for advice." She whispered it as she looked at me and then at Alex. We both nodded our heads in agreement.

We left the house about an hour and a half later and went our separate ways.

Chapter 24

Troy

Playing the Part

"Missing?" I looked at Ashley in shock as she told me that her sister Diana was missing. Of course I was acting and acting quite well I might add. We were sitting in the living room of her house. She had called yesterday and told me that it was important for me to come and see her today. So here I was sitting with her, Alex, and Jasmine.

"Yes, and there is no time to waste," Ashley said and then looked at me with urgency covering her face.

"True." I nodded my head in agreement.

"So can you help us, you know, get the people involved in this case to make my sister a priority and not a black loose chick who has gone missing?"

"That is going to be hard to do." I looked at her and then Alex and Jasmine. "I don't know who is on the case or what district has it. And even if I did, there wouldn't be anything that I could do about it. Once a case is assigned to a person or persons, interference can be treated harshly. I will look into it but that is about it."

"You're not serious are you?" She looked at me as if I was going to recant my last statement.

"I'm very serious," I answered. "I want your sister to be found and found alive but there is a conflict of interest here. You are my girlfriend. We have been seen together by other officers so it is a definite no-no." In actuality I really didn't care; shit I was the kidnapper. I knew the whereabouts but that was for me to know and them to find out. And they would find out, when I wanted them to find out. And by then it would be too late for them all.

"Ain't this a bit . . ." Ashley hopped up out of her chair and stormed into the bathroom and slammed the door. I looked at Alex and Jasmine because this behavior from her was new for me. I had never seen her this animated with anger or frustration.

"What did I say wrong?" I asked as I looked at Alex and Jasmine with bewilderment covering my face. I wasn't moved by the big outburst. This question was all a part of the act that I was putting on.

"Well, she gets like that sometimes. She is a little frustrated right now. She is used to being in control of situations and this one is testing her. I mean it is our sister you know. You sure that there is nothing you can do?" Alex asked.

"I will try my best to look into it. But I have my hands full with my own case. Which brings me to the next situation." I paused and looked toward Ashley's bathroom to make sure Ashley wasn't coming out. I needed to keep what I said right now between the three of us. "I need to see you two back down the precinct again. We have another murder on our hands and guess who was listed as the last contacted in her phone?" I looked at Alex intently.

"Who?" He looked a little nervous.

"I think you already know. But we can't discuss this here and this stays between the three of us." They both nodded their heads in approval.

"Let me go check on Ashley," I said as I got up from my chair. I walked down the small corridor that led to the bathroom and main bedroom.

"Ash," I called out as I knocked on the door. There was a brief silence before I knocked again. Still no response. I tried the doorknob but that too was a lost cause.

"Ash, babe, open the door. I want to explain myself some more. You have to know that I care greatly about your sister and I would do anything to get her back." There was still silence on her behalf. Her newfound attitude was pissing me off but I didn't want to deter her from thinking nothing but happy thoughts about me.

I heard the unlocking of the door and then slowly it began to open. I had on a bright smile as I peeked in and then walked in.

She sat back down on the side of her tub with her legs crossed and a perplexed look on her face. One thing about females that bugged me the most was the moodiness and uncontainable spasms of emotion.

"Ash," I said as I walked over to her and sat next to her. I was in very close proximity to her. I wanted her to feel and know that I was for her and all of her interests. "I'm sorry for being so stubborn and close-minded. I was a jerk a few minutes ago and I should have thought before I answered."

"True." She nodded her head as she looked at me with an expression I couldn't figure out.

"Look, I will try to pull a few strings to get a look at the evidence and who is working on the case. That is the best I can do right now. If there is more, then I will try my best to get that too. The last thing I need for you to be is mad at me right now when your sister is a priority." I loved that last sentence because it made her smile a bit. I was such a great actor that I was shocking myself.

"You were right." She nodded her head and then put her hand on my knee. "I should have been more considerate of your job and their protocol instead of getting pissed off because you didn't say what I wanted to hear.

I'm sorry for being such a hothead." She laid her head on my shoulder.

"Don't worry; if it was my sister who was missing I would be feeling the same way. We are going to get her back alive, believe me."

"Yes, I know." She nodded her head, but there was a little gloom that was mixed in with it.

"I said we are going to find her alive," I spoke with pep in my voice as I was trying to motivate her because she looked like she was carrying the world on her shoulders. "Say it with me."

"We are going to find her alive." We both said it with life and alertness. She was now smiling as she normally would smile.

"You feel better now?" I asked as I stood up.

She stood up as well and then said, "I'm so glad that you are in my corner and that you put up with me, flaws and all."

"No problem, Ashley. We all have our moments and then we move on. I got to see the crazy you a few minutes ago. I might have nightmares tonight but I'm sure I'll be all right after that." I snickered.

"Yes, I did lose it for a minute didn't it?" She smiled. She looked embarrassed.

"All is forgiven." I kissed her on the forehead.

"Thanks," she said as she, in turn, kissed me on the lips. "It means so much to hear those words. Too many people don't forgive. It will make you do things that you wouldn't normally do. And most of all it will control you. Forgiveness is the key to happy living. Thank you for forgiving me."

I can't even lie and say that her last statement didn't hit home for me, but it was too late for all of that now. The ball was already rolling and I was speeding toward the finish line.

"Let's get back out there so we can go over some type of game plan to push the awareness of your sister's absence."

We both walked out of the bathroom and into the living room to get started. The whole time I was sitting there planning with them I was counter planning in my head. She would never be found alive and I was going to make sure of it.

Chapter 25

Ashley

Beating the Pavement

Going to work was not happening at the moment. I called my boss and explained the situation to her. Like any human being she was immediately sympathetic to my request for time off and she even said I would get paid for it.

I knew my dad told me to not get involved in it, but that was like talking to a brick wall. I thought he knew it in the back of his mind, but he still said it anyway. I knew he meant it, too, but again, I was not going to have a half-assed cop pussyfooting around when my sister was missing. No, sir, not on my watch.

I was in my car with a stack of fliers that I had printed up. I had made a Facebook page for my sister. I even had a sign made of my sister's picture and information with it plastered on the side of my car. I wasn't playing. Everyone was going to be looking for Diana Black if I had anything to say about it. I had as many people as I knew posting and reposting on every social Web site that was well known and a few that weren't.

Social media was cool but good old-fashioned hand-to-hand was better to me. As I walked down the street and handed out fliers to any individual who passed by me, I thought about the times that I was on the opposite end of this scene right now. I would usually give a sad face and a weak smile to the person who was handing me the flier and then I went on my way toward what really concerned me. People didn't care until it happened to them. Murder, kidnapping, and violence were all experience teachers. I was getting taught right now that we as people took too much for granted and things in life could change drastically in a moment's time and most people outside of your family couldn't really care less and some inside as well.

"Have you seen her?" I said as I walked around a small shopping center a few blocks from where I had parked my car.

The older lady looked at me with concern as she spoke, "Such a beautiful young lady. Such a shame. Such a shame." She shook her head and wiped a tear that escaped her left eye. "My baby girl disappeared about two years ago and we still looking for her. I know how you feel, baby. I'm still looking for my baby. She turned twenty-nine years old yesterday and sure would have been nice to hold her in my arms. Lord knows I miss her."

She was crying pretty hard right now. I didn't know what else to do but I reached out and pulled her into a hug as she sobbed on my shoulder. Pretty soon I was crying as well. Her story made me think that I would never find Diana alive. I knew she didn't mean to make me feel this way but I was heartbroken right now. My little sister was missing and I was powerless to help her right now.

"Oh God, my baby!" The lady continued to sob into my shoulder. I pulled her in closer to me because I truly needed the hug right now as well. I was feeling all types of ways. This hug was everything right now.

After a few more minutes, she stopped crying and pulled herself away. "Thank you so much," she said as she wiped the tears from her eyes. "That was the first time I really cried like that. I am so ashamed that it had to be with a stranger." She laughed. I laughed a little as well.

"No problem," I said as I smiled at her. "We both needed a good cry right here and now. It felt good to let out some frustration. Do you have a flier of your daughter so I can make some copies and pass them out with my sister's information? It would kill two birds with one stone," I offered.

"You would do that?" She looked at me with shock on her face. "I . . . I don't know what to say. I have been doing all of this looking and searching by myself since I have very little family and now you come along and offer me help. I don't know what to say. I am so grateful that you would even offer it to me. Young lady, you are a very rare kind of special. Walk me to my car so I can get you a flier that is in the trunk of my car."

"Ma'am, that is no problem at all. One hand washes the other. We all need help in this world. I'm doing what I would expect others to do for me," I said as we walked and talked in the direction of her vehicle.

"Young lady, you must have some mighty fine parents to train you the way that they have," she said as we finally made it to her car that was only a few blocks away from the shopping center I was in at first.

"Yes, my parents did a great job in training me. Plus, it's right to help someone else, especially if we are in the same type of situation."

"You are so right, baby," she said as she opened her trunk and pulled out a stack of fliers for me to hand out for her. My mouth hung open at the sight of the picture on the flier. It wasn't what I expected.

"Are you all right, baby?" She looked at me curiously. "Something wrong?"

"Miss, this is a damn dog's flier," I said because I was instantly pissed off at this lady's foolishness.

"What do you mean?" She looked confused. "This is my daughter."

"I'm not passing out no damn dog pictures with my sister fliers. Are you crazy?" I looked at her as if she had two heads and a dog's tail. I knew I shouldn't have been so disrespectful to her but I was overheated with attitude right now. I mean this lady had me in the middle of public crying on my shoulder all because of a damn missing dog.

"But I thought you said that you would help me out. I really miss her." She looked at me all pitiful looking. I was not falling for it though.

"That was when I thought it was a damn person I would be looking for instead of a hot in the ass dog." That dog was probably chilling somewhere in someone else's house and away from her crazy ass.

"So you not gonna help me?" she asked again as if I was going to change my mind.

"Miss, look for your own mutt," I said as I walked off, pissed, in the direction of my car.

Chapter 26

Alex

Surprise Guest

I pulled up to my home and exited my car with fatigue in my steps. I had walked for miles today passing out fliers in search of my sister. I had taken off of work for a few days so that I could focus my attention on what was more important right now, but that didn't stop Lance from calling me asking me what I was going to do about the blackmail thing he had going on. I was waiting on Wallace to call me back with the information and help that I needed to get this thing to disappear for him. I still wanted to be broke off financially for going above the call of duty as an agent. His PR person was supposed to handle his messy stuff not me but with this type of situation I know he had very few options for help. I had to figure out how to approach him for a cut of the hush money. That little sissy boy wouldn't be getting any but I damn sure wanted some. I knew it was wrong but hey it was better than playing the lottery. Both this and the lottery were once-in-a-lifetime chances and I wasn't asking for a million dollars. A hundred grand would be nice. I could do a lot with that. Anyone could actually.

"Dude, you not that tired. I know they don't work you that hard," a voice said from behind me as I was about to enter my building.

I knew the voice well but it couldn't be who it sounded like.

"Man, what are you doing all the way over here?" I smiled as I greeted Wallace, my deceased biological father's lover and also one of my best friends. I embraced him with a tight hug and then pulled away. "Dude, you cut your hair?"

"Yep, it was time for a change." He smoothed his hand over his low-cut hair. I had to admit he looked good without the dreads.

"Man, you came all the way back to Baltimore from California to help me out?" I looked at him in wonder. It was amazing how true friendship could cause you to react in unwavering dedication to another person.

"I would love for you to think that." He laughed. "Truth is a friend of mine passed away and I flew back here to help his mom bury him properly. It was a plus that I get to help you out as well."

"I'm sorry to hear that, Wallace, but I am glad you are here. Come on in the house with me so we can catch up a little."

We both walked in my apartment. He sat in my living room while I went into the kitchen to grab us something to drink.

"Man, this is a real nice place you have going on here." He nodded his head as he spoke. I sat down on the chair diagonally from him and handed him his drink. "Thanks, man." He opened it and took a quick swig of it.

"Yeah, it a great place to be," I agreed. "Nothing like having your own place."

"That is true," he said. "So why are you getting in so late? I know that you are not working this late at the office."

"No, not at all." I shook my head. "Truth is, man, my sister Diana is missing and I have been out for a quite a few hours handing out fliers trying to find her."

"Man, are you kidding me?" He looked at me in disbelief. "For how long?"

"Close to four days now I think."

"What are the police doing about this?" He looked at me with concern.

"They are doing their best and have been updating us daily, but it is still no leads on her whereabouts or cause. It's like she disappeared into thin air."

"This is crazy. I had a few friends working for me down at a few of the precincts when I was doing dirty business a few years back. I will make a few calls to see if they have been doing all they can do to get this case solved. We all know how inept cops can be at times." He shook his head.

"True." I nodded in agreement. "Not to change the subject but who got the restaurant while you are gone?"

"My mom and Rebecca are watching over it until I get back. It was a little hard to let it go and fly here but you have to do what you have to do when a need of a good friend or friends arises."

"Dude, you are amazing," I said in awe of his last statement. "Who talks or thinks like you?"

"Nah, I try to treat people the way I want them to treat me. It has been working for all of this time with a few exceptions so why stop now? My life is good and I am healthy with family all around me. Who could ask for more?"

"I see why James liked you. You are straightforward, honest, and you are passionate about peace. Who wouldn't want a mate like that?"

"Well, I was lucky to have him for the time I did as well. I really can't complain."

I could tell that he was getting a little emotional about that subject so I moved on back to the other subject that I asked him about a few days ago. "So you think you can help my client out of this situation without it being illegal?"

"Alex, I have a few ideas and I will call in a few favors from some specialists in this area of expertise. I'm not going to say that it won't be illegal but I will keep you clear of the drama. Did you get the information that I needed?"

"I sure did. I have it in the other room. I'll be right back." I hopped up off of the chair and made my way into my den to retrieve the information for Wallace. It felt so good to have help. Doing stuff by yourself was the pits.

I walked back into the room and handed him the papers with information on them. After he looked over the papers he nodded his head and a smile came over his face.

"I can't lie and say I won't enjoy this last caper of drama before I head back home and back to the normal life."

"Yes, there is nothing like a good rush of adrenaline to get the heart going," I said as I remembered some of our adventures out in California.

"We sure did have some adventures going on a few years ago didn't we?" he said as if he had read my mind.

"Yes, but some of that was out of this world. Some of the stuff I still can't believe to this day." I laughed as I thought about Rebecca and Grace and the fact that they had so many people fooled for so long.

"Yeah, I'm still adjusting in some ways but all in all life is good." He nodded his head.

"Wallace, you are welcome to stay here if you want. I don't have a piece coming over tonight so you are good." I laughed.

"Let me find out you have your father's libido. He was insatiable at times in the bedroom." He laughed.

"Well, let's say the apple didn't fall that far away from the tree." I laughed again.

"I hear that. Be safe. It's some crazy chicks out here. And to answer your question I wasn't planning on staying anywhere else." He laughed again and so did I. I loved Wallace and our friendship. It was free and comfortable.

We stayed up for a few more hours catching up before we went to bed for the night.

As I lay in bed and before I drifted off to sleep the fact that Troy needed to see me and Jasmine back down at the police station drifted to the forefront of my mind. There was so much going on that I almost forgot about it. How was I going to get out of this one? I couldn't tell anyone about it, especially my parents, because I didn't want to worry them at this time with Diana's kidnapping on the forefront. I closed my eyes and prayed that it all would work out and work out for my good. Right now drama was escalating in my family and we didn't need anything else to happen.

Chapter 27

Jasmine

Committed

Here I was sitting in my doctor's office waiting for her to come back to tell me that I was pregnant. I had goose bumps up and down my legs and arms, from both nerves and the chilliness of the room. It was a little over a week from the day that I had sex with Alex. I was glad to be sitting here, ready to receive some good news. I looked around the room at all of the advertisements and things that hung on the wall. One had a picture of a man and woman with who I would assume was their baby and loving smiles on their faces. I thought about my mother and then my father's face popped into my mind. I smiled because I thought of the possibilities of my family-to-be; then a heavy feeling came over me all of a sudden. The room grew colder by the second and I rubbed my hands over the sides of my arms to warm them but it was to no avail. I doubled over and rocked back and forth with my arms clutched across my chest. I was having a panic attack. Everywhere I looked I saw my mother's head as I looked around the room to find a safe place to hide.

"Stay away from me. Stay away from me," I moaned in terror. I couldn't believe that this was happening to me now.

"Is everything okay?" The door to the room I was in swung open quickly. The look on the nurse's face was one of panic. "I heard yelling."

"Yelling?" I looked at her like she was crazy.

"Yes, yelling." She looked at me with even more bewilderment. "Like someone was being hurt in here."

"You must have heard wrong." I gave her attitude with my statement. "Where is my doctor with my test?"

"She will be with you shortly," she said as she looked at me a few more seconds and then she closed the door and left.

"Shit." I banged my hand into the side of head. "Got to hold this shit together. I can't lose it now. I'm too close to my goal. Please, God, give me some more time. All I need is a few more years. Please, God." I pleaded with God to be merciful. I wanted to have a family.

"Is everything okay, Jasmine?" My doctor came back into the office with a piece of paper in her hand. My eyes followed it and not her around the room as she took a seat in her chair.

"Yes." A smile of hope was covering my face. The look on hers was hard to read. I wanted to tell her to get on with all of the questions and give me my damn results. This whole situation was pressing my patience to an all-time low. *Come on with it, bitch!*

"I am happy to tell you that you are with child." She smiled as she spoke.

"Really?" I was asking to be sure. I knew she wasn't lying but I wanted to make sure this shit wasn't a crazy hallucination or something. I had my moments. I wasn't oblivious to my situation just not focused on that shit right now.

"Yes, really. You are having a baby."

"I . . . I can't believe it." Tears welled up in my eyes and began to fall down my cheeks. I brushed them away but they continued to fall.

"Well, believe it. In nine short months you will be having a nice bundle of joy. Was this something that you wanted or was this an accident?" she inquired.

Did this bitch call me a whore on the sly? I know she didn't. She couldn't have. Maybe I was overreacting. Yes, I was overreacting. She didn't want to be a victim. I was sure of it.

I almost said that I killed a few bitches to get this baby, but I didn't. That probably would have freaked the shit out of her. She was this petite white woman probably in her early fifties.

"It was planned. We have been trying for a few months now and finally today it is all coming true." I sniffed back tears as I spoke.

"So the father knows you are here?" she asked.

Okay, this bitch is really pushing it with these questions.

I kept my cool and answered, in case I was wrong. "Yes, he had to work. But he really wanted to be here with me. He is going to be so happy to find out about our baby. This is the start of a great life for us. We got married a few months ago, bought a new house and car, and now this. Life is good for us right now. I can't wait to tell him. This the first of many."

"I'm so happy for you. Being a mother is so rewarding. I look forward to walking with you during this process. I am going to need you to follow up with me in a few weeks to check out the progress. Here is a prescription for some prenatal vitamins and few other things that you will have to take to keep you and the unborn child healthy," she said as she handed me a few slips of paper.

"Thank you so much. I am going to enjoy this process as well," I said as I hopped off of the table I was sitting on. I was ready to go and spread the good news. My first stop was my daddy's grave. I had to tell him the good news.

***

"Daddy," I said as I kneeled down in front of his headstone, "I miss you, Daddy." My voice trembled a little. I smoothed my hand over the embossed picture of him on the headstone. My daddy was so handsome. Just like Alex.

"Your little girl is going to be a mommy. You're going to be a grandpa. Can you believe it?" The silence drove me wild. I knew that there would never be a reply but I still hoped for one.

"Daddy, I wish that you were here and that she was in there instead of you. Why did you stay with her, Daddy? Why didn't you leave her? Why did you let her take you away? You were supposed to be here. You let her kill him! You let her kill him!" I cried out toward the heavens.

I stayed at the gravesite for a few more minutes as I got out the tears that I hadn't shed since my mother killed him all those years ago. They were long overdue. I drove home in gloomy quietness. I entered my home alone for the last time yesterday. Today I was officially not home alone.

Chapter 28

Troy

Suspicions

I sat in my office, at my desk, deep in thought. I was going over the events of the day before yesterday. Alex and Jasmine had made another trip down to the precinct where I worked for some investigative questioning. I have to be honest and say that I was totally perplexed with the fact of this last girl's murder at the club and these two being in the same club on the same night and the fact that his number was found in the victim's phone once again. My chief was pressing me once again with the progress of resolution and I was sure he was being pressed by the district attorney's office. Seven murdered females over the period of a year wasn't a high priority on the list of importance in Baltimore but it was getting close. I was under the microscope and now the guy who was supposedly working with me on this case was smitten with me because I wet my dick in his hole the other day. I didn't include Ashley in this last inquiry because I didn't know how she would respond or act. I, for a fact, knew that Alex wanted this to go away, and quietly I might add. After sitting down with these two I had some very promising suspicions on the brain. This was how the meeting went down two days ago:

There was a knock on my office door. I was on the phone with one of Ma Dear's doctors being filled in on the progress since I hadn't been down to see her in a few days. I had a lot on my plate and she wasn't a priority at the moment.

"Come in," I called out, while still having the phone pressed to my ear. I was intently listening to the latest prognosis while I signaled the two to come in and have a seat. They both sat down; Alex had a concerned look on his face and Jasmine had a smile plastered on her face. I noticed she always has a smile plastered on her face when Alex was around. All other times she was simply straight faced. Not mean, but unemotional. I didn't get to be around her much but I did notice that one irregularity.

Anyway, I was on the phone for but a minute more before I ended my call and focused my attention toward them alone. "Nice to see you guys today," I said as I shifted some papers around on my desk and retrieved the file I was going to need for questioning. I was being cordial because I was in a strangely fair mood today. I really didn't openly and honestly care about them per se. They were filling a space for the moment. "I want to let you know that this inquiry is being recorded for the purpose of this case. Would you like to have a lawyer present and postpone this so that they can be here with you or shall we continue as is?" They looked at each other for a moment before Alex spoke.

"I'm good. I know that I am innocent," Alex said with confidence. It was a macho type of confidence. I looked over at Jasmine for her response.

"I'm glad we could make it to see you today too; and no, I'm sure of my baby's innocence," Jasmine said almost like she was overcome with joy. Not a typical emotion displayed here in a police station and under these circumstances.

"Well, as I was telling you guys the other day, there has been another murder, but this time it was in a public place and you two were in the same establishment." I filled them on some specifics.

"Really?" Jasmine gasped and put her hand over her mouth in shock. Alex had no reaction. I guessed he was shocked. Or holding in his reaction for fear of incrimination. I didn't know yet.

"Yes, this is a female who had Alex's name in her phone and he was the last person she contacted that night." I looked at both of them simultaneously and then at Alex to see if he was going to give any type of response.

"Alex, he talking about that girl you came with. She was your cousin right?" she looked at him and asked. She looked like a pot brewing to a boil.

"Yes, that is who he is talking about," he said as he shifted in his chair. He looked nervous. I would be too if I were in his situation right now.

"Alex," I said and then paused as I pulled out a transcript of a few of the texts that had transpired between the deceased and him. I handed them to him. "These are a few of the text messages that were sent between the two of you in the hours before her demise. Can you explain them to me?" A part of me was laughing at him on the inside. I was a little concerned how Jasmine was going to take this news, since she was his girlfriend and she didn't respond too well to this type of information the last time he was in the office with her. But something was off about their last time in this office. These two were a mismatched couple. They say opposites attract but I wasn't sure in this case. They didn't fit together in my eyes.

"Explain?" He looked at me. I could tell he wasn't sure how to answer me.

Before he could answer Jasmine snatched the paper and got an eyeful for herself. "I want to be the mother of your children," she read out loud. You could see the anger rising up on her face. "I am going to enjoy blowing your back out trying to conceive them," she continued to read. "I can't . . . I can't . . . believe you would do this to me, to us." She rubbed her belly and trembled as tears fell from her eyes. "How could you?"

I looked at her in shock, not knowing that she was carrying his baby. It threw my suspicions out of the window. She rose from the chair she was sitting in and made her way into the corner of my office as she did the last time. Her low sobs could be heard in the silence of Alex and my silence.

"Shit," he exclaimed. He got up from the chair and walked over to where she was standing. "Jazz, I'm sorry. I know I said that the last time was the last time, but I need help. I need your help for us. I can't do this without you." He hesitantly touched her shoulders after he spoke. "I didn't mean what I texted her. I was trying to get laid. I have an addiction. I have a problem. Please forgive me. You mean the world to me, baby."

She said nothing as she continued to cry. He stood there waiting for her response. I was waiting as well. Not for the same reasons. I wanted to get on with this inquiry and exclude him as a suspect again.

"You promise that you are going to get help?" she asked as she finally turned around. Her eyes were bloodshot. It crumbled my suspicions about them being fake lovers.

"I promise. For us and the baby." He pulled her into an embrace and again they shared a long, smoldering kiss that even made me jealous. I wondered what his lips tasted like. I shook the thought from head as they finally finished.

It didn't take long for them to become chummy again and even clasp their hands together when they sat back down in front of my desk once more.

"So can you two explain your whereabouts during the time at the establishment?" I asked.

"She was with me the whole time at the club except when she had to go to the bathroom. I'm not the type to follow a chick to the bathroom so that is where I assumed she went." Alex answered with conviction in his words. "In fact, Jazz saw her go into the bathroom with her own eyes."

"Is that true, Jasmine?" I asked and waited for an answer.

"Yes, I saw that trick go into the ladies' room as I was coming from the bar. She looked sloppy drunk," she said with a smile back on her face.

"Did you see her come out of the bathroom?" I asked Alex.

"No, she was in there for a minute. I gave up on waiting. She wasn't my girlfriend. She was an easy lay. I went home alone. I mean Jasmine drove me home. I was intoxicated." He looked over at her and smiled. "My baby always has my back." It made her smile even harder.

I bypassed the sentiments of love with, "So now that we have this on file, I can officially remove you from the list of suspects once again. And my advice to you, Alex, is to stick to one girl so you won't end up in here again. At least not for this."

"I will." He looked at me and then at Jasmine. "For my baby I will."

"Since we have that out of the way, you two are free to leave. And I appreciate your cooperation. Have a great day." I got up to shake their hands. They did the same.

"I hope you find this heathen who is doing these hideous crimes so us girls can feel safe walking the streets again," Jasmine said before she closed the door to my office.

Not long after they left there was another knock on the door. "Come in," I called out.

The door opened and Nelson walked into my office and closed the door. "Who were those people who left your office?" he asked without even saying hello.

My head was lowered, looking at a document. "They were people I was interviewing for the case I'm working on," I answered, not caring to look up at him. Professionally I had no respect for him, especially after he let me fuck him the other day. Personally he was a good fuck and I would do it again for sure. Thinking about his tight little hole made my dick throb in my pants.

"I thought that you were supposed have me in here when you did interviews?"

I looked up at him, finally. He had on an angered look. Like he wanted to fuck me up. I didn't care. He was a peon to me. "I was, but I didn't." I looked at him in the eyes. He was a handsome guy. It made my dick harder.

"I'm tired of you not taking me serious. I'm supposed to be working with you."

"You are working with me." I looked at him up and down, with only one thing on my mind. "You remember the last time you were in my office?"

"Yes." He nodded his head.

"That was work." I stood up from my chair with a very noticeable hard on. I rubbed it and then squeezed it. "And I need you to work again."

"But that's not why I came in here." He sounded frustrated, but his focus was on the imprint of my dick. He was a slut and he knew it.

"It is. Now go and lock my door so we can get some work done," I commanded.

He followed the instructions like I knew that he would. "Now come over here and work on my erection." He did as he was told. I pulled out my erection and waved from side to side as he made his way to his knees.

His mouth felt really good as he took all of me in it.

"Mmmm," I moaned as low as I could. He was damn good at this work. "I'm gonna have to tell the boss to give you a raise for putting in such good work."

He was supreme in his sucking skills. It was like he was trying to ease my woes through the head of my dick and into his mouth. I was going to let him, too.

"Damn, boy, who taught you how to suck like this?" I asked, rhetorically. He continued to take me all the way in his mouth with his face slamming into my pelvis. I was getting weak in the knees as he crammed all of me in him time after time. It didn't take long for that one good thrust to send my woes and seed down his throat.

He pulled away and looked up at me. His face was a mixture or satisfaction and disappointment. Maybe he wanted me to plow his ass but there was only time enough for a face fuck.

"Don't worry. I'll fuck you next time." I zipped up, walked back around my desk, and sat down. He was still on his knees in front of my desk. I began to shuffle some paper, ignoring his presence.

"What about the case?" he finally got up off of the floor and asked me. "What if the captain asks me about the case?"

"I'll e-mail you all of my findings so you can be caught up. Other than that, the only time I need to see you is when I need some wet mouth or ass. Got it?"

"Yes. I got you." He still looked disappointed. If he was looking for love he needed to move on. I wasn't the one. He was a good lay.

I laughed to myself as I came back to the present. "That was a good day for me." I was mainly talking about the fuck and crossing Alex off my list as a suspect. That still put me back at square one for suspects. I still had my suspicions about Alex and Jasmine's relationship. I mean it looked and seemed legitimate. But I for one knew how to fake a good relationship, because I was doing it now. Something wasn't right but I still couldn't put my finger on it. I would be paying closer attention from now on for sure.

Chapter 29

Ashley

Milk Carton Mischief Too

My sister was still missing and it was driving me insane with worry. It'd been well over a week and there was still no progress. We had passed out hundreds of flyers and posters and there were no solid leads. A few people thought they saw her but it was only a girl who resembled her. I ran up on a few chicks like they owed me something thinking that they were her. I had gotten a few hours of sleep in the last couple of days and that was the same for most of my immediate family. We were all insane with worry. Every passing moment read more into a negative outcome. No one wanted to admit it but it was growing rampant in the midst of us. No one was really saying much about anything else but Diana. My mother was a supreme basket case right now. She lay in bed grasping a picture of my sister as a baby. My father was aloof and absentminded, which he never was.

Right now I was actually at my parents' house sitting in the living room with the television on. I had a laptop beside me with Diana's Missing Person's Facebook profile up at all times. I was waiting for the next lead.

"Hey, Ash, any luck today?" My little brother Shawn came into the living room and sat on a chair near where I was. He looked like he was worn out as well. My mother had been super protective of all of us since Diana's disappearance. I couldn't blame her either. I had been sleeping over here for the last couple of days so that any news that came anybody's way could be worked on as a family. Truth was I wanted to be near my family. Something like this definitely brings a family back together. Not that we were divided. Everybody was busy with their own lives and the things that they were focused on.

The only one who was not staying here with us was Alex. His buddy Wallace was in town and staying at his place until he went back to California. My mom and dad felt good that Alex was with Wallace; they knew that he was in good hands. Alex would check in from time to time to get a heads-up. He and I both were on leave from work because of all of this.

"Nothing as of late," I said trying to give off some positive vibes. "How are you holding up?"

"I'm doing well as expected in this type of situation. I've been posting a lot of things about Diana on all of my social sites. Still no progress. I can't believe that she is missing. It was like yesterday she was sitting where you are right now and we were talking about how hard college was and things like that. Now she's not here."

Those two were around the same age so I knew that he was feeling the void more than the rest of us, with the exception of our parents.

"Look, keep your head up and a smile on your face. That girl is a fighter and I know that she is going to be back safe and sound. I have a good feeling she'll be back."

"I sure hope so, because I can't take this type of living. I can't stop thinking about the 'what ifs,' you know?" He sniffed back some tears. He was trying to be strong. He was the spitting image of my father and I knew he was so much like him. He was trying not to show weakness like most males did, but it was hard to do when a sibling or family member had gone missing.

"I know I have been going over them as well. Nothing we can do about that now," I said as I blinked back some tears myself.

"She asked me to go with her that night and I declined because I wanted to get some studying done. Can you believe that? I chose studying over going to the club. Who does that? All of this could have been avoided if I was with her." He hung his head low after he spoke.

I got up out of my seat and squeezed next to him. I pulled him close to me by his shoulder as he sobbed into my chest. I had never seen him cry like this ever. He was really feeling it. I even allowed some tears to fall.

"Look, we can't be in here crying and mourning yet." I pulled him up and looked him in his eyes. I needed to be comforted as well, but as the big sister I was the one to do the uplifting right now. "We need to get back to work."

"Okay." He wiped the tears from his face with his shirt. "You right. She wouldn't want us acting like this right now. She would be hustling if it were one of us."

"Right, now go get us something to drink and snack on while I check some of these sites for any leads."

He got up and made his way into the kitchen. I did as I said I was going to do and sat down in my original spot. My phone began to vibrate on the cushion next to me. I picked it up and looked at it. It was a text from an unknown number. It read: Meet me at Grandview Ave and Holiday Rd if you want to see your sister alive again. Come alone. If we suspect any setup going on she will die. Again, come alone.

Every hair on my arms and legs stood up. I was in disbelief of what I was reading. Everything in me was telling me to have someone follow me. But I didn't know if this was serious. I had watched too many television shows and movies with this type of setup and the person given the instructions deviated from the instructions and someone ended up dead. I didn't know what to do. They didn't ask for money or any type of ransom. Only for me to show up alone.

I got up out of the chair and headed for the front door. As I got there my mother came down the steps.

"Ashley, where are you going?" she asked with a little panic in her voice. I wanted to tell her everything, but I couldn't take a chance on my sister's life. I had to go alone.

"I'm going to the store real quick. You want something?" I lied with a bright smile on my face. My mother looked a hot mess and I didn't want to stress her out even more.

"No, but take your brother with you." She looked toward the kitchen as Li'l Shawn came out with a few things in his hands.

"Take me where?" he asked as he walked up on us.

"She's going to the store and I don't want her to go alone. Get your jacket so you can go with her," my mother instructed him. He did as ordered.

"No. I want to be alone for a minute. Ma, I promise that I will be careful. I want to be alone right now. I need some time to think outside with some fresh air," I pleaded.

"You sure?" Li'l Shawn asked as he looked at me and then at my mother.

"Yes, please, y'all. I'm going to be fine," I assured them.

"Well, okay." She reached out and pulled me in for a hug. It was a tight and warm hug. One that I needed. I was getting ready to go into the unknown. I prayed that this was the real thing and not a game. I didn't have time for games. My pressure was up as it was and I was liable to do anything at the moment.

I gave Li'l Shawn a hug and then made my way out of the door and into my car. I pulled off and looked into the rearview mirror as my childhood home faded into the distance.

Fifteen minutes later I was at the location that was designated in the text. My mind raced as I thought about the possibilities of this situation. Was my sister alive? Was this a trick? Who texted me? Why did they snatch my sister?

It was nightfall now and I was getting scared. Ten minutes had passed and I was still sitting in the car waiting on whomever texted me to show up with my sister. The neighborhood I was in was a really quiet one. It was close to a body of water. It looked like a manmade lake or something. I had never been to this part of town before.

My phone vibrated in the passenger seat. I picked it up. It was another text. It read: We know that you have arrived and that you are alone. Good job. Someone is going to walk by with a black hood for your head. Put it on and pull the string at the bottom to make sure it is secure. Unlock your door. Make any type of noise and your body will end up in the lake nearby along with your sister's.

I began to shake uncontrollably at the thought of being thrown in a lake, or dying, period. I didn't like this situation at all. I had come too close before and here I was again. What was I supposed to do? Pull off and leave my sister's fate in the hands of some crazy person? I couldn't do it.

It didn't take long for the person to come alongside the car, tap on the window, and hand me the hood. I couldn't see if it was a man or a woman because they had on a hoodie that hid most of their face. I placed the hood on my head and pulled the string at the bottom. Almost immediately the door to my car was opened and I was pulled out of the car and placed in what I could only imagine to be the trunk of a car.

I didn't know how long I was in the trunk of the car but it seemed like forever. But soon the car came to a halt and then I heard the trunk being opened. I squirmed a little in defiance and the person reached to take me out of the trunk. They stood me up; they had my hands and legs bound so that I had depend on them to hold me up. My heart raced as I felt the hood being lifted from my head. The bright light in the room caused me to shudder and my eyes closed. The next thing I felt was a wet cloth being placed over my mouth and me getting weak.

Chapter 30

Alex

Ride Along

I called Ashley earlier today, to check in on the status of my still missing sister, Diana. There still were no leads. Ashley was over my parents' house posted up like she had her own private task force base set up. She was going hard for my sister and I wanted to be there with her but I definitely had to take care of this situation while Wallace was in town.

"So you are sure you want to be here while this happens?" Wallace looked over at me in the driver's seat of my car. A few years ago it was the opposite and I was in the passenger side asking questions.

"Yeah, man, I want to see this situation get handled." I nodded my head.

"Seriously, Alex. This is some stuff that is highly illegal and immoral that is about to go down. Shit that is going to stay with you forever."

He looked at me intently as if I was going to change my mind. I had seen some things, unnatural things, so whatever was going down tonight probably would be nothing.

"Wallace, man, I'm grown. I can handle my own. You know this already, so save me the speech and let's get this shit done so I can move on and focus back on my missing sister."

"Cool. I'm giving you a choice. Remember there is no turning back after this," he said as we pulled onto a quiet residential street. It was very close to midnight. There were a few cars parked on the street along with a dark-colored van. There was no noise being made except for nature.

"See that truck up there? That belongs to a friend of mine. He and his buddy owed me a favor from back in the day. They in there now rounding up your client's blackmailer," he said as he pointed in the direction of the house.

"A buddy of mine retrieved the address of the black-mailer from his Internet provider. The guy I knew who helped me with all of that tried to break all of that down to me over the phone but I didn't really care about it. He said it was a very complicated process and he had to dig deep because the little blackmailer was a "smart li'l fucker."

Anyway, Wallace and I sat in the car for a few more moments before we saw two dudes, masked up and in all black, carry what looked like a body out of a house and into the van and then quickly pull off. Wallace signaled me to do the same.

My adrenaline was racing as we followed this van for about twenty-five more minutes. When we finally did stop it was in a desolate part of town that I had not been to before. I was amazed at all the places that you could do unsavory things at in Baltimore. We watched the dudes carry the body out of the van and into a building that looked like an abandoned auto mechanic shop.

We waited a few minutes before Wallace instructed me to follow him. "Come on man, let's go inside." He exited the car and I did the same. As soon as we got to the entrance of the building he stopped.

"What's wrong?" I looked at him, wondering why we had stopped at the door.

"You sure about this? You can stay in the car if you want. No one will think any less of you." He looked sincere in his approach as always. It made me think more respectfully of him than I did before.

"No, I'm all in. Let's go."

He didn't say anything else as he opened the door and I followed him inside. The place smelled of rusted metal and car fluids. As soon as we went into the main part of the defunct shop we saw the two guys standing over the limp body on the ground. The two guys still had their masks on. They threw a black book bag at Wallace without a single word said. He reached inside and pulled out two masks identical to those the other two guys had on. He handed one to me and I placed it over my head as did he.

At this very moment I knew what it felt like to be a thug or to at least resemble one.

"Stand back there and watch these dudes do their business," Wallace instructed me. The big, brawny guys moved in silence as they pulled out a camera and various other things. They left the shop and returned with another large bag that looked like another body. Anticipation and discomfort both enveloped me like a flickering light switch.

Pretty soon they had a scene set up that was out of this world. It made me look at the underworld of violence, crime, and illicit activities very differently.

I watched as they undressed the guy who was blackmailing Lance and then they stuffed some type of pill down his throat while he was still unconscious. On the mattress they had the black bag spread out across it. They unzipped it and sure enough it was a white naked man with his manhood tied to appear like he had an erection. I gagged a few times at the sight and the smell was strong, making me think that this guy was freshly killed. I couldn't believe I was watching this take place. Wallace had backed up to the position that I was standing at as well. He was focused on the situation at hand.

Soon they laid the extortionist next to the body. All of this happened in a matter of twenty minutes. Not long after they laid him on the mattress the extortionist began to show signs of movement.

Then all of a sudden he began to stand up and move around like he was a zombie of some type. It was weird because he was walking around with no place to go.

"What the hell did they give him?" I peered over and asked Wallace.

"It's a strong hallucinogen that makes the person taking it very manageable. He will do anything that is told of him."

"Wow," was all that I could say as I watched one of the guys whisper into the blackmailer's ear and then all of a sudden he went over to the dead person and positioned himself over the body and began to have intercourse with the body. His moans of pleasure filled the room. I was flabbergasted at what I was seeing. All of this was being recorded for retaliation purposes. The guy was riding the corpse as if it was a real live person. He moaned and gyrated with abandon. I turned away several times though and heaved until I threw up the contents of my lunch and dinner.

"This is some wild shit," I said as I leaned over in Wallace's direction.

"I gave you the choice to not to come," he said back. I didn't say anything back.

One of the bulky guys signaled to the other guy to cut the recording. Which he did. I was relieved that it was over.

"I'm so glad that's over," I whispered as I leaned over into Wallace's direction once more.

"It's not over. Keep watching."

All I could think was what more could they do?

Then one of the guys came in our direction. I flinched a little because he looked like he was coming in my direction, but he walked right past me and out of the door. A few short moments later he walked back in with huge-ass dog with a muzzle on his face. The muzzle didn't keep me from being fearful of him getting loose. I wasn't a dog lover. I didn't hate them but they weren't on my list of things to interact with or have.

Anyway, pretty soon they removed the dead body and then whispered into the guy's ear again; this time he got down on all fours and they placed the dog behind him. The dog hopped on the guy and I bolted for the door. That was my breaking point. Wallace joined me as well.

"I can't believe what is going on in there is actually going on in there," I said as I shook my head in shock. I should have stayed in the car like he instructed me to do when we got there. Even though I didn't see it all, I still knew about it and that was something that you couldn't forget no matter how much you tried.

"Again, I told you to stay in the car, but your nosey ass had to be in the mix of things." Wallace laughed a little. I did as well. Not at the situation but the truth about my nosiness. They say curiosity killed the cat.

About fifteen minutes later, one of the two guys came out of the vacant establishment and walked over to the car we were in while it ran idle. The guy walked to the passenger side of the car and handed Wallace the recorder and then walked away. No words were exchanged.

I pulled off headed back toward my house. As I drove all I could think about was if this was really worth clearing up Lance's mess and getting him out of the hot seat. I was party to a very crazy scene back there. Wallace didn't lie when he said that it would be immoral and unethical. That mess was something I didn't want to ever do or see again. He didn't say anything else during the ride and neither did I.

We pulled up in front of my home and I turned off the car and sat there for a moment.

"You all right, dude?" he asked as I looked straight out of the window into the distance.

"Yeah, I will be." I tried to smile but I couldn't. I thought about my missing sister and broke down crying in the car.

"Lex, dude, the guy had it coming to him. No need to cry about it, man. Move past it." He tried to comfort me with words.

"I'm not crying about that." I sniffed back some tears and wiped my face with the back of my wrist. "Man, my sister is missing and that scene back there could have been my sister. Man, somebody could be doing some wild shit to my sister right now."

"Lex, your sister is going to be all right. She will be back in your parents' home safe and sound in no time. Believe me. Don't give up, Lex. Your hope keeps her alive."

"Wallace, this life shit is hard. It's some messed up people in this world and they will try to mold you into one of them if you don't watch your back."

"Alex, you are right. I have seen some crazy things and done some even crazier things as well, but I ask God for forgiveness and I move forward. I'm not an angel and never proclaim to be one. I like people to be treated fairly. I go about it differently than most and for the most part this was my last action of a vigilante. No more save a

Negro antics for me. I'm too old for this shit. A brother ready to go to bed now." He laughed and so did I.

We both got out of the car and entered my building. We both showered and lay down for a good night's sleep.

Chapter 31

Jasmine

White Walls

Here I was driving on I-695 getting ready to take the exit that led to Spring Grove Mental Hospital. I had taken half of the day off today to take care of this situation. I was sweating profusely through my hands. So much so that my hand had slipped from the wheel as I made a turn. I hadn't seen my mother in close to ten years. She had been housed in this facility for a long time. I had made this trip on several occasions only to turn around as I neared the entrance. Today would be different. I was going to get to the front door and inside to see her. This was a monumental moment in life for me and even though she may not have even known me or remembered me, I was going to do as Ashley had suggested and tell her the good news.

I pulled into the designated parking area, turned off the car, and breathed out an aggravated breath of air. She was my mother so why was I having all of this anxiety right now? I grabbed my pocketbook off of the passenger seat and exited the car. I took small steps as I headed across the parking lot that led to the facility. I watched a few people exit and enter the facility. I wondered if they were patients or visitors. The closer I got to the building the more my heart raced.

I entered the building; a whoosh of cold air hit me in the face. It caused chill bumps to rise on my arms. I had made an appointment to see her a few days ago as they requested so they could prep the patient for the visitor.

"How are you doing today?" I asked the front desk attendant. "I have an appointment today to see my mother."

"Name please?" she asked plainly.

"Jasmine Richards," I answered. She typed a few keystrokes into the computer and then looked at me.

"We have no Jasmine Richards in our system."

"Oh, you meant the patient's name." I laughed a little. She didn't. "Her name is Rachel Richards."

"Thank you," she replied while entering a few keystrokes into the computer. "Go to the door on the left. Wait for the buzz and then open and proceed to the security checkpoint," she instructed.

I did as I was instructed and proceeded through the door and in a few short steps I was at a security station that was equipped with two guards and a metal detector. I proceeded to unload my things onto the conveyor belt and then walked through the metal structure. I was relieved that the alarm didn't go off. I retrieved my personal belongings and was instructed to go in a waiting area at the end of the hallway.

I entered the medium-sized room that had several tables spread apart. Everything in the facility was white. There were three attendants in the room for security purposes. There were also a few other visitors sitting across from patients having conversations. Some of the patients looked a little disturbing. It unnerved me a bit to be in the presence of some possible unstable but medicated people.

It didn't take long for two attendants to bring my mother in and sit her in front of me. She looked a little worn in the face. Her graying hair was long and in a neat ponytail. She was still pretty like I remembered her to be. The nervousness subsided in me some as I stared at her face and body.

"Hey, Jazz, baby." She smiled as she spoke. "I'm so glad you came to see me today. I thought you would never come to see me after all that went down. I loved your father." She looked away from me briefly and then returned her eyes toward me.

"I didn't come here to talk about that, Rachel," I said with plenty of attitude.

"I know, I . . . I . . ." she stammered. Tears started to fall from her eyes. They were too late for me. "I never got a chance to apologize to you. Tell you I was sorry."

I looked at her with pain and anger boiling up inside of me.

"I can see that this is hurting you by bring this subject up. I'll leave it alone."

"Thank you," I replied. "Sorry is not going to bring him back."

"I know," she said as she lowered her head. "I wished things would have turned out better than it did that day."

"Stop it," I said with a gritty hush-toned voice. "You knew that you were unstable and yet you still didn't take your meds. He didn't even know you were unstable. Neither of us did. You brought this on yourself. He was good to you and you killed him. You took his life away. My life away."

"You are right." She solemnly nodded her head. "But what you don't know is that your father was a womanizing whore. He cheated on me mercilessly. He pushed me."

"He didn't on cheat you. Your nagging ways drove him to seek comfort in the arms of other women. You know it was your fault he cheated. You nagged him into the arms of other women." I knew all about my father's so-called cheatings. He was stressed out from her and her unnerving displeasure with everything.

"Jasmine, you sound like you are in denial. I know the symptoms of instability. I knew that I would pass it on to you. I feared this. Have you ever gone to see somebody to help you out? Someone to talk to about your mental problems? You are as unstable as I was at your age. You don't look like you are unstable but I know it's lurking around in that head of yours. You can't hide it for long before it gets the best of you." She looked like she had pity for me on her face. I hated it.

"I'm nothing like you, you crazy bitch." I leaned across the table and said it to her so no one would hear me. "Nah thing."

"Ummhmm." She laughed. "I bet."

"Anyway." I bypassed her laugh. "I'm not here to talk about any of that. I'm here to give you some good news. I didn't want to tell you but I was talked into coming. Now I regret coming."

"Good news!" She perked up in the chair, causing one of the attendants to look in our direction. She instantly calmed down. "They letting me out of here?" she asked with hope all over her face.

"Nah, bitch, as long as I'm alive you will be in this crazy coop. Believe that," I said and then laughed. I was at all of her appeals for release and I performed so much in protest every time I thought they were going to release her.

She didn't find it funny at all. I didn't care. "No, I'm here to tell you that you are going to be a grandmother."

"Me a grandmother?" She looked shocked.

"Yes, you." I smiled proudly. I smiled because on the inside I knew that I was going to be a better mom then she ever was and I knew that my husband, Alex, wouldn't need to step outside of our marriage because he would have all he needed in me.

"Nooooooooooooooooooooooooo!" She hollered out and then fell out of her chair and onto the hard floor. "Don't let her have it. Don't let her continue this bad blood that runs through our veins. Don't let her have that baby. She should be in here with me. Don't let her leave. Don't let her leaveeee." The attendant quickly scrambled to get her together and sedated her with a needle in the arm.

She yelled and hollered so much that it caused the room to be flooded with staff and the entire facility to be put on lockdown.

I walked out of the facility with a smile on my face. I was happy to let her know about her grandchild. Her ass thought I was crazy like her. I walked across the parking lot with my head held high.

"I am very sane," I said as I got in my car and looked at myself in the mirror. "I got this all in control." I pulled off of the parking lot and drove toward my home.

It was kind of late when I got home, but when I did I wanted someone to talk to about my visit with her so I dialed Ashley's cell phone number and went straight to voicemail. I figured she was with Troy and didn't want to be disturbed or she was handling some business about her sister. Either way, I would meet up with her soon to give her the details.

Chapter 32

Troy

Family

Here I was on my way to check on Ma Dear. I had a lot on my mind as pertaining to the plans I had in place. Things were coming together nicely. I had Diana on lockdown and no one had a clue that it was me who was behind her disappearance. I would go and check on her almost every day to make sure that she was still functional, which was a task in itself. Taking care of another person was work especially when it wasn't on a voluntary basis on their end. She was a fighter for sure. She didn't make it easy for me to care for her; kicking, screaming, and going limp were all a part of her routine when I went to feed her, bathe her, or let her use the bathroom. But it would soon be worth it all.

I pulled into the facility and made my way into the building. I checked in and walked to the room where Ma Dear was being held. As soon as I walked in the room I received the shock of my life. She had another visitor. It was a family member I didn't see too much.

"Well, well, well," this nuisance of a person said to me as they shook their head at me. "I don't get to see you much since you have your own life and career. You nearly fell off of the map. I was about to put out an APB on you so I could see what you look like."

"I've been busy," I said dryly. "Getting some things done in my life. Making me a priority. You should know all about that since you have moved halfway across the country like your other siblings and started doing your own things. Why are you here anyway?"

"Dear brother." He laughed and placed his hand over his heart in a feminine manner. He was a queen like no other. He was in full drag but to average person you wouldn't know that it was a he and not a she. He was very convincing. "Why must you come for me? I came in peace to see Ma Dear."

"I bet," I huffed and folded my arms against my chest. He turned his attention back toward Ma Dear and completely dismissed me.

I walked around the room to the other side of Ma Dear's bed, to the unoccupied chair, and sat down. Ma Dear was still in and out of lucidness.

"Troy, Ma Dear keeps on mumbling obscenities and this man's name. Who is James Parks?"

"I don't know who that is. She has been in and out for the last few weeks, but you haven't been here to know that though. Calling the facility to check on her progress is not the same as being here," I scolded him.

"So you've been checking up on who comes and goes here?" He looked at me with displeasure.

"I am her next of kin and in charge of her state and estate. She is my business. I'm the only one here for her. Power of attorney, baby!" I answered. "So yes, I keeps tabs on everything and that includes you and the rest of my siblings' interactions here."

"For you to be the youngest you think you know everything and have everything under control. I could come back, swoop in, and take the reins of all of this and leave your ass on the sidewalk to cover up with the curb." He snapped his finger in true feminine form.

"You can keep all of that and besides I have the paperwork. You would be wasting your breath and time. We both know you are not going to do any of that or you would have done it already. Nice try though." I sat back smugly because I knew I had the upper hand.

No one knew about my siblings and I liked it that way. The life of an only child was a privileged one. You see I was the youngest of five children. I was the last one in the house and the only one left in Maryland to care for Ma Dear. She chose me to exact revenge for the family, mainly her, and I was all for it. I didn't need any interruptions from the peanut gallery. They had their lives and moved far away. They had their resentments and reasons for leaving and I had my resentments and reasons for staying.

"Whatever." He twisted his hand in the air to dismiss what I said but he knew I spoke the truth. He was passing through and saving face. He couldn't care less. He wasn't on my mother's list of favorites anyway. He was competition, but that was business for another time.

"When are you leaving?" I asked.

"Why?"

"Because I wanted to spend time with Ma Dear alone. Like I usually do."

"I will be out of here shortly and on a plane back home to my man. He been blowing up my phone for me come on home anyway. I came here to make an appearance, see Ma Dear, and leave."

"Cool." I got up out of my chair and rounded the bed. "See you when you leaving." I left through the door and went into the waiting room right outside the room to wait for him to leave.

It didn't take long for him to make his way out of the room. "Bye." He waved his hand without even really looking my way.

"Better to see you going than coming," I shot back before he got on the elevator.

I went in to check on Ma Dear and to let her know that her plans were moving ahead swiftly. I was not sure if she fully understood what I said but she nodded her head when I told her.

I left the facility and decided to call and check in on Ashley and her whereabouts. As soon as I got to my car and sat in the driver's seat I pulled out my cell phone to call her. I dialed her number and it went straight to voicemail. I did this several times with the same results. I took it as a sign that she was handling business and could not be contacted at the moment. I decided to go check on Diana real quick and then make my way home.

Chapter 33

Ashley

Kisses Down Low

I awoke to a feeling that I knew all too well.

"Mmmmmm," I moaned involuntarily through my duct-taped mouth as I tried to get my eyes to focus. I felt cold and naked. I tried to move but I was restrained once again. As soon as my eyes could focus the sight before me made me pissy mad. I couldn't believe what I was seeing and feeling. I squirmed and shifted in the bed I was in, trying to get loose, but it was useless.

I looked down at a totally naked Antoinette going to town with her tongue deep within me. She was trying her best to make me orgasm but I wasn't having it. I couldn't say that it wasn't feeling good though. She was a beast with her tongue game. I was in for the fight of my life. It didn't take a rocket scientist to figure out that she set all of this up. This bitch kidnapped my sister to get to me. Who did something like that? A desperate person that's who. That shit was genius, too. I was glad that my sister would be okay, too. I had to find a way out of this shit.

"Hey, baby girl." She looked up at me and smiled. My eyes said "fuck you." But she didn't care. I knew it. "You taste so good. I'm going to make that pussy cum a hundred times before I stop," She said as she stuck two fingers in me and wiggled them around. I lifted my pelvis off of the bed in rejection. That didn't deter her though; she pushed me back down and dived in with her tongue once again.

Her work down below sent shudders of ecstasy throughout my body. I wasn't trying to enjoy it but I couldn't help it. She was giving it to me.

"Oh shit, girl, you taste good. And you wet as hell. You wanted this didn't you? I know you did. I can tell by the way you are squirming and twitching," she gloated with my juices around her mouth.

"Mmmmmm." I thrashed and tussled again in defiance. I was like a tied-up bull trying to get loose.

"Calm down, girl. I am working as fast as I can. We don't have nothing but time." She laughed.

I couldn't believe this bitch had me tied up and licking my pussy. You would think that there wasn't any free pussy around. She could get some from damn near anywhere especially in Baltimore. Pussy was prevalent. There were plenty of bitches who would let a bitch kiss them down low for a good nut and nothing in return.

"I can't hear you moan. I want to hear the pleasure. I'm going to untie your mouth but if you start acting up I will get my licks while you are unconscious again," she said as she got up off of the bed and walked over to the top of the bed. "Are you going to be a good girl?" she asked.

I nodded my head yes.

She removed the tape from my mouth and the first thing I did was take in a gulp of fresh air. Breathing through the nose was cool but the mouth was a lot easier.

"What the fuck am I doing here, Antoinette?" I said as she walked away and my breath returned to a regular pace.

"You know what I said. I said I loved you and I wanted you back. But you wanted to play games so I had to make the choice for you," she said as she looked at me from the end of the bed.

"So you kidnapped my sister to get some tied-up pussy for a few days?" I looked at her with anger. "Who does that type of shit?"

She laughed before she spoke, "Ashley, I don't know where the hell your sister is at. I used the information to get you where I wanted you and ta-da, here you are tied up with your legs gapped open. All you had to do was say yes and all of this shit could have been avoided. I can't believe you were trading me in for a meat stick. What's wrong with my tongue?"

"Are you fucking kidding me? You don't know where my sister is and here I am tied the fuck up so you could use me as your sex slave. Really? Bitch, you are fucking loony tunes crazy. Your ass is not going to get away with this. You're a fool to think otherwise." I was seething with anger. Here it was my sister was missing and this bitch had added me to the list. What kind of shit was this? I could only imagine what my parents were going to be thinking when they found out that I was now missing too. They were going to have to put my mother in a psych ward for sure now.

"Oh, baby, I'm going to get away with this for sure. No one knows where you are. I chucked your cell phone in the water where you left your car. No fingerprints. I used stolen plates on a truck to get you here in case the area was being watched. The phone I used was a replica that I bought off of someone. You were a fool to use your phone number on the fliers to find your sister. But you didn't know any better though. I lucked up with that one. And so here we are now. All you had to do was give us another chance and it wouldn't have to be like this."

"Bitch, you are absolutely crazy to think that I will ever be happy with you."

"Oh, happy is not needed. I'm about to move us out of the state and to our new home. Far, far away from here.

We are going to be together even if it is by force. Pretty soon you will get used to it and broken down to where I want you to be. It's inevitable."

"They are going to come looking for me. They will never stop looking. My family loves me. They will go broke trying to find me. I feel sorry for you because you have to stoop down to this level to get someone to be with you. What kind of a poor excuse of a woman are you?" I taunted her with every word that I spoke. I wanted her to see that I would never voluntarily or involuntarily love her. She was delusional.

She walked over to a dresser that was in the corner of the room and opened the top drawer. She fumbled for a few minutes before I heard something make a clicking sound. She turned back around and faced me.

"Ashley, this will speak loudly for me. See if I can't have you then no one will. I will kill you and myself. Easily," she said as she aimed the gun with a silencer attached to it at my head.

I didn't flinch nor did my eyes wander. I had been here before. But would it end the way it had before? Only time would tell.

"Then I guess that is the way that it's going to be," I said, unmoved.

She squeezed the trigger and fired.

Chapter 34

Alex

Not Again

I was startled out of my sleep by the ring of my phone. I threw my legs over the side of the bed before I reached for the phone. I picked up, looked at it. It was my brother Li'l Shawn.

"Hey. Wassup?" I asked in anticipation of some news about my missing sister Diana. My stomach started to flutter in anticipation. Good news or bad news; that's what I wondered, feared.

"Man, you better get over here and now. I have no time to explain. Get here," he said in an almost hushed voice.

"Okay." I immediately hung up the phone and searched the room for something to put on. I quickly washed my face and made my way into the living room where Wallace was laid out on my sofa.

"Yo, Wallace." I shook him gently so that I wouldn't scare him out of his sleep. That wasn't a good feeling at all.

He woke up in an instant and asked, "Everything okay?"

"I don't know, man. My little brother called me to go over my parents' house. It sounded urgent. You rolling with me or are you going to chill right here until I make it back?"

"Nah, man. I'm with you," he said and then he proceeded to put his clothes on. He made a quick trip to the
bathroom before he followed me out of my house and to
my car.

I pulled off quickly so that I could get to my destination
with haste. My mind was all over the place. I didn't know
what to expect right now.

I arrived at my parents' house in fifteen minutes on a
regular twenty-five-minute drive. Wallace looked at me
in fear as I drove with reckless abandon on the highway.
I was on a mission, but I should have taken my time
because an accident wouldn't help the situation, good
or bad. I almost hopped out of my car as I got out and
walked around to my front entrance. Wallace wasn't too
far behind me as I opened the front door to the house and
walked in.

I headed straight for the living room as most of our
family interaction was held there. As soon as I entered
the room everyone's attention was focused on me. My
mother, who looked a hot mess, hopped up and ran over
to hug me around my neck. I looked on as my father was
obviously shook up as well. My brother Shawn had the
look of death on his face. That sinking feeling of despair
and dismay covered the face of Jasmine, who was also in
attendance. My grandmother looked like she wanted to
pass out as well.

"What's going on?" I asked as I pried my mother from
around my neck.

"She's not answering her phone. She's not answering
her phone. She's not answering her phone. She's not
answering her phone." She kept on repeating it as she
looked at me.

"Who's not answering their phone?" I looked around
the room for an answer from anyone.

"You sister went out yesterday and that is the last time that we've seen her. Her phone goes straight to voicemail every time we call it," my father said as he stood up. I hadn't seen my father cry in a long time, but today, right now, he was letting them fall freely. It broke my heart to see him like this.

"Didn't she say where she was going when she left?" I asked as tears welled up in my eyes. My twin was missing and I was almost instantly grief stricken. The flashback of the last time that she went missing in California flowed through my mind. She almost didn't make it out that situation and now here we were in the same situation again. *What the hell is up with this family and kidnappings?*

"No, she said that she wanted to take a walk and do some thinking," Li'l Shawn said. "I knew I should have gone with her like Mommy said. She wouldn't be missing if I would have gone with her," he said as his voice began to tremble.

"Look everyone, calm down," I said in as calm a voice as I could. "Let's not jump to conclusions. We don't have any information yet. Has anyone called Troy to see if she was with him or if he has talked to her?" I asked as I looked around the room. My mother had eased her way back across the room and into the arms of my grandmother. My youngest sister, Brittany, was huddled up next to my mother. She looked like she had been crying as well. My whole family was messed up right now.

"Yes, he said he tried to call her as well but he got the same result that we did when we tried. He said he would be here as soon as he can get off," Jasmine said from the corner of the room.

"Okay, let's get the police involved in this and see what they can do to help the situation."

"We did that. They said that they will combine the cases since they are related. They also said that they would add another person to the case but they couldn't make any promises," Jasmine answered.

I looked at my father for some help, but he was looking out into space like he was lost. I was hoping he could pull some strings with a friend or something but I was assuming that would have been one of the first things he would have done already if he could, so that was out.

"Wallace." I turned and looked at him because he was standing behind me with his hand on my shoulder. "What else can we do?

"Let's track her cell phone. See where that leads us to." He looked at me with hope in his eyes.

"Okay, let's start there." I nodded my head.

"Here's her laptop." My sister Brittany hopped up and ran it over to me.

Chapter 35

Jasmine

Spectator

I sat in the corner and marveled at Alex as he went into action. I didn't know the fine brother who was next to him, but they both looked like they were about to get the business going as it pertained to finding Ashley. I was definitely going to be a ride along anywhere they had to go. Alex immediately went to work on Ashley's laptop.

I looked around the room at all of the family who were in the room. It was quite amazing to see the cohesiveness of the family. You had Mr. Black's mom consoling his wife. She was in very good control of her emotions right now. You could tell she was the stable head of the family. Even after all that the family had been through.

Then you had Mrs. Black who was an emotional wreck right now. Her hair was all over her head in a disheveled mess. She was still in her wrinkled pajamas and housecoat. Bloodshot eyes and a tearstained face also accompanied her present persona. Her family was going through some very trying times right now and she was feeling it. I felt her pain.

Next you had the baby of the Black family, Brittany, who was so full of energy and love right now. She was going back and forth to the kitchen for drinks and snacks for everyone in the room without a murmur of complaint.

It was astonishing, because at her age most children were usually not that focused on the needs of others. But she was doing it up right now. It made me happy to see it.

There was also Li'l Shawn, the middle child. He was sitting next to Mr. Black and he was rubbing his father's back. It, too, was mesmerizing to see. This family was close knit and even through the rough times they were here for each other and focused on the needs of all who were around.

A tear escaped my eye as I tried to blink them back. This was the epitome of a family. It was what I wanted. Needed. Strived for. I looked down at my stomach and smiled. *Soon I'll have a family like this one!* I couldn't wait for my baby to make its entrance. I had a little less than nine months to go but I was ready. I had my stuff in storage and my plan for my family was a go. Alex needed a little more persuasion to give us a go. I was waiting for that opportunity to arrive. My heart throbbed at the thought.

"Both of my babies are gone!" Mrs. Black let out a bellowed moan. It caused everyone in the room to turn their attention toward her. She started to shake and then fell limp in her mother-in-law's arms. Mr. Black hopped up and went to his wife's aid.

"Is she okay?" I asked in concern as I got up and moved closer. Since I was the caregiver for her mother and a private nurse I immediately went into caregiver mode. She looked like she had died. That was how limp she went. I had never seen anything like it in my life. I was consumed with concern. I reached back to the chair that I was sitting in and grabbed my purse. I quickly fumbled in my bag for what I needed and handed it to Mr. Black. He had a look of relief on his face as he placed the smelling salts under his wife's nose and she slowly came back around. The look on everyone's face was a collective look of relief of tension.

"I found the signal to her phone!" Alex jumped up with a smile on his face.

"Let's get on it and track it down," the guy who came with Alex suggested.

"I'm ready," he said as he headed for the door.

"I'm going too," I said as I gathered my things and trailed behind the two closely. They were moving rather quickly. It was expected.

We all hopped in the car and sped off in an unknown direction. I had to say that my mind and heart were racing as Alex drove through the streets like he had lost his mind. I could only imagine what was going through his head right now. He and Ashley were quite close. As close as they say twins can be. You know, like they feel each other's pain and emotions at the same time.

The car came to a halt in a matter of fifteen minutes. We all hopped out as soon as we saw Ashley's car. We were in a residential area with a manmade lake type of body of water in close proximity of the car.

Alex and the other guy ran up on the car and immediately opened the door. I watched from a close distance while they searched the car feverishly.

"Shit!" Alex got out of the car and huffed. "Her phone isn't in here."

"Let's check the trunk," the cute older guy suggested. The look on my face as they went into the car and popped the trunk was one of pure torment. I didn't want to see my best friend being pulled from a trunk. It would have been too much to bear.

They popped the trunk and thankfully there was nothing in there but a spare tire and a few other car essentials. I immediately felt at ease until Alex looked at his phone and then turned his attention to the body of water that was in the area. My stomach plummeted once more from the thought of my best friend's body being in it. This was too much to deal with.

"It says that the phone signal is coming from the body of water," Alex said with dejection in his voice. The look on his face was one of pure and utter fear as I walked up on him and stood beside him.

"It can't be," I said with tears in my eyes. The thought of it caused my legs to lose their strength and I almost tumbled to the hard ground beneath me. If it weren't for Alex's quick reflexes that caught me in time, I would have had a few nasty bruises to nurse.

"Come on now, Jazz, let's not jump the gun on this one. It could be her phone in the water and not . . ." He didn't even finish his sentence before he was letting tears fall from his eyes. He had me cupped from the midsection of my back and close to him as he spoke. I felt so safe in his arms. He looked at me in my eyes as he spoke. It felt so good to be in a man's arms. Especially, one who was in high regard on your list of potential mates.

"I know." I sniffed back some tears and snot. "It's too much to bear or think about. But I can't help but think about it." I put my hands on his firm chest as I got myself together and pulled away from him. I was mildly aroused as well.

"I need to head back home so I can brief my father on this situation. I don't know how but I have to tell them it in a manner that doesn't make it look like it looks." He looked at the other guy and then at me.

"Wallace, Ashley's car keys are still in the car. Do you think we should take it back home or leave it for evidence? Even though we potentially could have tampered with some evidence already?"

"I say leave it here. The police will want to look at it in its present state. And as far as evidence goes, I don't think we did that much tampering for them not to be able to find pertinent clues to the case," Wallace said with confidence that made me feel at ease.

"Okay, let's head back home and get the police involved."

All three of us hopped back in the car and headed back to the house to give everyone the heads-up on the situation. I was trembling as we got closer and closer to the house. This was like one of those scenes when you got a knock on the door from the army letting you know that your loved one who was fighting in a war was killed in action. This was not shaping up to be a very good time for me as an expectant mother. This type of stress could cause me to miscarry and I didn't need that right now. But I ignored it and as soon as we got to the house I followed the two guys as they walked to the house with everyone still pretty much in the same spots as when we left them. They looked at us with anticipation.

Wallace was the one who eventually broke the news to everyone and most of the room looked on in somberness as he spoke. Mrs. Black was not too thrilled with the news and it led to another fainting spell and her having to be brought back around with smelling salts again.

Chapter 36

Troy

Not on My Watch

I sat at my desk with my emotions running on high. I had gotten the call earlier in the day that Ashley wasn't anywhere to be found and now I got the call that said they found her car and her cell was under a few feet of water. The stress of my boss coming to me every other day with the progress of this case of these murdered women was starting to get to me. I felt a throbbing headache on the horizon soon if I didn't get my pressure down and fast. I really needed to get the hell out of here and see what the hell happened to Ashley. I was furious that someone was trying to up me in the offing of one of my victims. Ashley's ass must have pissed somebody off and now they were gunning for her like I was along with the other two. I had to do some work to get this stuff done so I could make my exit. I needed to get on top of this situation.

A knock on my office door caused me to become even more frustrated. "Come in," I bellowed.

My fuck boy partner on the case walked through the door. He had a smile on his face and something in his hand. "I haven't heard from you in a few days. I came in for some work." He sat on the edge of my desk with a smug look on his face. I looked at him with irritation written all over my face.

"This is not the time," I said looking back toward what I was working on and not at him.

"Oh, I think this is the time." He hopped off of the desk and waved a manila envelope in my face. I reached for it and he quickly pulled back and moved a distance away from me. My interest was now piqued as I look at him in wonder. What was in the envelope that he thought he could use as leverage to get some dick from me? He looked good in the outfit he had on and his behind look ripe for the picking.

"Right now is not the time to be playing games with me. I'm not in the mood and you could really get hurt by fucking with me right now." I stated the facts as I got up from my chair and walked in his direction, stopping short of two feet from him.

He looked at me for a few seconds and then laughed. "What I have in this envelope will change your life and maybe the case, if you give me some of that wood on a permanent basis. Me likey." He laughed again. I still didn't find him funny but I did need to relieve some stress and there was no better way at the moment then busting a nut.

"You have a deal," I said as I complied. I unzipped my pants and let my dick do what it did best. He gravitated toward me like a mouse to cheese. He fell to his knees instantly and took me into his mouth. He was a master at his head game. I reached for the envelope but he had as good a grip on it with his hand as his mouth had on my dick at the moment.

I palmed the back of his head and relished the good head that I was receiving. I felt all of my problems drain out of my balls, getting ready to release into his mouth.

"No, no, not so fast." He grinned as he pulled up. "I want to feel that wood on the inside." He unbuckled his pants and pulled his pants down. He had on no underwear, which let me know that he was trying to get fucked today. He pulled out a condom from his back pocket and slid it to me through his now-gapped legs. He was a show off for sure. I liked the show. I strapped up and slid in.

A low sigh of "ahhhh" slipped through my lips as I felt his warm walls gripping my dick. I eased out of him partially and then slammed into with force. A small yelp came out of his mouth. I felt it to be pleasurable and warning to not do it again. I didn't want to alert anyone to what was going on.

I slowly and methodically pumped in and out of him so that we both would enjoy it and not get caught in the process. In a few quick pumps, I exploded inside of him and pulled out. I reached for the envelope and pushed him away in the process. He lost his balance and Nelson tumbled to the floor. After a few minutes, he got himself together and sat in the chair in front of my desk.

I sat down at my desk and opened the manila envelope. It contained a disc. I looked at him in curiosity. "How long have you had this disc?" I asked.

"I've had if for quite some time. I was waiting for the right moment to give it to you. I held it longer since you were being such an ass about everything. I have a copy of it so you won't try to screw me out of credit for this case if there is something credible on it."

"Did you review it?" I looked at him as I placed the disc in my laptop and waited for something to happen.

"No, I wanted to see what your reaction would be before I watched it."

I thought that it was stupid for him to wait for me to watch it but I let him do him. "Do you know what it is?" I asked not looking at him.

"One of the owners of the club brought it in. I'm assuming it was footage of the club."

He was right. It was footage of the club but I wanted to be alone as I watched this video. "Thanks for the help. You can exit my office. I will make sure you get all of the credit due to you." He looked at me for a few more seconds before he got up to exit my office.

"Until next time," he said as he exited my office.

I continued to survey what was on the disc until it got to a pivotal point and my mouth hung open in shock and amazement. I was now viewing footage of Jasmine going into the ladies' bathroom and then the murdered chick going in right after her. Only one of the ladies exited the bathroom a few minutes later. I quickly paused the disc and fumbled through the papers on my desk for the autopsy of the deceased girl. I looked at the probable time of death for the victim and the time stamp on the video and almost lost my composure as I was excited for finding this information at the time that I did. This would help me in my personal life and in my professional one. Jasmine just became the missing piece to my puzzle.

I exited my office with the disc in hand. I hopped into my car and made my way over to the Black residence to get clued in on Ashley's disappearance. This was a huge glitch in my plans. It made me feel uneasy and angry as I made my way over to the Black residence. I hated interruptions especially in my plans.

Chapter 37

Ashley

Close Call

My mouth hung open in shock as I looked over my shoulder at the bullet hole that was in the pillow next to my head.

This chick wasn't playing.

"Cat got your tongue now don't it?" Antoinette looked at me with confidence in her eyes.

She was right. I was speechless at the moment. Naked and speechless.

How in the hell was I going to get out of this shit? It actually looked like she was going to get away with this. I was going to be this bitch's love slave for life. She was planning to run away with my ass and disappear off of the map. I had watched too many crime shows to know that she had this shit planned out. A fear grew up inside of me like never before.

"Antoinette, what about your friends and family? Aren't they going to miss you? Aren't you going to miss them? I mean up and moving like you plan to do is not a good look. People know I'm connected to you. I'm missing and you missing means they will put two and two together and we would have to be on the run forever. Are you really trying to go that route? That's some rough living. On the run and all of that. Sleepless nights. Ducking and dodging. Disguises and all of that mess. Are you really game for all of that?"

"I'm about that life, so it's no biggie to me. I've been in these streets before. I've seen things and survived even more. I got this shit all worked out, so you better get used to this here tongue all over your body from here to eternity."

Shit! This chick is some lunatic type of behavior. I might have to play along and see how far that gets me.

"Antoinette, I have to use the bathroom," I said as I squirmed around a bit in the bed. She had me tied up pretty good. Her ass must have gotten a Girl Scout badge for tying knots and shit as a kid. I mean I had been tied up before and this was very close to the last time. I was hoping my father would come busting through the door at any moment now and rescue me like before. But I felt like a cat that was on his last of the nine lives he was given.

"Sure, I got you covered." She went to the bathroom and seconds later she came back into the room with a female urinal.

I was too through. She really did have all of this planned out.

"Told you I got this down. We are going to be good together. If you act right."

"Antoinette, I have to do number two. You know, shit and piss." I looked at her with a smirk on my face. She looked stumped.

"Look, I'm only going to say this once." She looked at me in the eyes as she untied one of my hands. "You try any shit and I will clean your clock. Because I love you don't mean I won't blacken that eye. I want an obedient mate. Got it?"

"Yeah, girl. I'm not going to try anything. I get what you are saying and I'm all for it." I smiled like I believed the words that I spewed out.

"For real?" She looked elated. She wasn't ready for me. I wasn't going back in that bedroom and being tied back up. I couldn't do it. I was a fighter and if I had to take a few blows to get out of here that was what I was going to do.

"Yeah, Tony. You got me feeling some type of way when you was licking me down under. I felt a real connection like before. It felt like love." I almost burst into laughter as I fed her some of the most make-believe bullshit I ever did speak. She was slurping up every word I spoke as truth. I wasn't no fool though. She could be egging me on as well.

She finally finished untying me and she helped me off of the bed. I turned and looked at the soiled sheets that were on the bed.

"Antoinette, could you change the linen on the bed? I don't want to lie back down in the same filthy juices. Even if they are my own."

"Girl, I am going to lay this tongue on you one more time before I go to sleep. I'll change them afterward."

I rolled my eyes in disgust, because she wasn't giving me any room to get away from her. She was going to make this difficult. She walked me to the bathroom and watched me as I sat on the toilet bowl.

"I can't use the bathroom with someone watching me," I lied. "Plus, it's not ladylike for someone else to smell my personal business." I looked at her and smiled. I was trying to be adorable. I needed something to work.

"Girl, all shit stink. Plus, I got you for life. This will be the first of many so let that load go so I can get back down to them skins." She laughed.

I laughed too, but it was more of an "I hate this bitch" type of laugh. She didn't know it though.

Who knew that doing some outrageous things in your youth could lead to this type of drama? It goes to show that you never knew who you really sleeping with until you broke up with them. All hell broke loose when you on breakup status.

I used the bathroom and then I wiped myself clean.

"Antoinette, I have to take a shower if you going to be going down on me again. I have to." I looked at her with urgency written all over my face.

"No problem. Turn that water on and hop on in," she said as she handed me a wash rag. "The body wash is already in there."

"Are you going to sit here and watch me bathe?" I asked, already knowing the answer.

"Sure am." She nodded. I sucked my teeth in disgust.

"I need a shower cap. I don't want to get my hair wet," I said before I stepped in the shower.

"Damn, girl. You one high-maintenance chick," she said as she fumbled in one of her vanity drawers. "Ashley, I don't have no shower caps. My shit is natural. I don't need one."

"Well, you are going to have to get me one or a plastic bag. Something. I refuse to shower without it." I was dead serious when it came to my hair. My hair was natural too, but I had it flat ironed. It's bad enough she had me in there in that bed sweating and twitching without a scarf on my head.

"Shit." She stomped as she exited the bathroom. She quickly turned to leave me with one more work of discouragement. "Remember. I will beat that ass real good to show you I'm not playing. I'm serious."

"Go on, Antoinette. I'm not trying to go anywhere. Get me something to cover my head," I said with a half of a smirk and half of a smile. She left and I quickly scanned the room for something, anything, that would aid me in my escape. There was nothing. I mean she had nothing that I could use as weapon. She was on point. The only thing out in the open was a plunger and I didn't know what in the hell I could use that for other than the toilet it was next to. I was pissed as I had to wait for her to come back with a Walmart bag to cover my head.

I covered my head as best I could and showered. I was pissed beyond belief. I was stuck in this situation and nowhere in sight was help to get me out.

As soon as I exited the shower, I dried off under supervision and then she escorted me back to the bed and tied me back up like I was when I first awoke to the situation. And yes, she did as she promised and went down on me again. I didn't want to like the orgasm she gave me but my body gave in. I drifted off to sleep shortly after that hoping that I would wake up and this all would be a dream.

Chapter 38

Alex

Lost

I couldn't help but say that I felt lost without my twin.
I really, really missed her. I missed Diana as well, but
Ashley was a part of me, my other half. I felt in my soul
that she was still alive. I was so relieved to see Troy walk
through the door of my parents' house yesterday evening.
He had the look of grief on his face. It didn't take him
long to get into action and call in a few favors before they
had some scuba divers combing the body of water where
Ashley's cell phone signal was located. Everyone was
super relieved as we watched them come back up with the
phone and no body.

But that was the beginning of our problems. If she
wasn't in the water, then where was she? We had nothing
to go by yet. I was hoping that they could get something
from her phone records. Because right now there was
nowhere to look. And no persons of interest. Who could
be behind all of this?

One other thing that perplexed me a little was how fast
Troy went into action when it came to Ashley versus what
he did for Diana's disappearance. I understood that was
his girlfriend but Ashley asked him to give it all he could
when it came to helping find her sister and he did just
about nothing. He made a few promises but that was as

far as it went. Now he had helicopters and scuba divers looking for her. That didn't sit right with me. Maybe it was me overreacting or overthinking in the time of all of this chaos. He did get us this much help for Ashley. Maybe he couldn't get the help at the time that he asked for it for Diana. That's what I would believe for now. I was sure that I was overthinking.

"I don't know what else to do or think about, Wallace." I looked at him as we sat in a small restaurant so that we could quickly grab something to eat. I wasn't eating much food these last two weeks. Troy was with us but said he had to use the bathroom. We were also here to come up with something that we could go on to help us get some clues as to who may have wanted to hurt either one or both of my sisters. For all we knew, they both could be tied up together somewhere with some unknown freak. It also floated through my mind that my sisters could both be victims of this person who was killing all of the other chicks over the last few months. It was all so unnerving. What did all of this have in common?

"Well, this is so mindboggling to say the least. I am unsure of what to do next. I will say that you should be careful not to go anywhere alone. Whoever is doing these things may have you on their list as well."

Troy walked back to the table we were sitting at as Wallace finished his last statement.

"Yeah, you are so right about that." I nodded my head in agreement.

"Right about what?" Troy asked and looked at me in wonder.

"Wallace was telling me that whoever was behind this may have me in mind as well so I should try not to go anywhere alone," I informed him.

"That is some sound advice, but I don't think that you will be kidnapped by this person." He spoke confidently.

"Why do you say that?" Wallace asked.

"Because men getting kidnapped in this city is not likely as it is for a women." He spoke as he looked at Wallace and then to me.

"I still say be cautious, Lex." He looked at me as if he wasn't thinking about what Troy said. "You could be the exception."

"Well, I will agree on that," Troy said.

"So what information do you have already that we may have overlooked?" Wallace directed his question to Troy.

"Well, we retrieved the last text message from her service provider that gave her instructions on where to go to get her sister. But that leads us right back to where we are right now. We can assume that the person who kidnapped Diana also did the same thing to Ashley. That's how the investigation will be treated, as a combined case. Also, none of the neighbors noticed anything different in the area on that evening of the occurrence. I'm waiting for a neighbor to come back home from an extended trip overseas. There was a private surveillance camera on his property that may have caught something."

"Really?" I perked up with enthusiasm and hope.

"Let's not get our hopes up though. This could be a dead end as well. We have to cross our fingers and hope that he comes back in time to help us. I am not going to sleep until my baby is back in my arms." Troy looked away trying to hide the hurt that he had written all over his face. He really loved my sister. I was so glad that she had him in her life. It was a welcomed change.

"We are going to hope for the best and claim victory for both of my sisters. They will be found alive and well." I smiled with inner peace that came out of nowhere.

"Yes, I know that your sisters are fighters like their father was. They are going to be fine. I know it." Wallace nodded his head with confidence and spirit that was always present when he showed up on the scene.

"Look, I have to go and take care of some personal business. Fill me in on any progress that comes up and I will be sure to do the same thing."

"I sure will," I said as Troy got up and I did as well. I reached out for a handshake and pulled him in for a hug. He was like a brother now and there was no denying it.

We disengaged and he left the restaurant as me and Wallace went over the final details of helping my client, Lance. The video was being prepped and ready for delivery to the blackmailer. I had a peek at it and all of the things that they added to it and it was amazing what technology could do.

The blackmailer would be shut down for life and Lance would be free to sleep at night once again. I had decided to let the money issue go and not press him to be paid for the help. I didn't want that kind of karma to come my way when I least expected it. I didn't need that with all of the drama that was going on right now.

We left that restaurant and made our way back to my parents' house to check on my parents and the rest of the family.

Chapter 39

Jasmine

Desperation

I had a busy day today. Half of the day I tended to my clients and the other half I had spent with Black family looking for Ashley and Diana. Now I was sitting on my sofa watching one of my favorite reality television shows with a glass of wine and some dinner I picked up from Boston Market on my way to the house. I didn't have the energy to cook anything today. The drama that was going on right now in my life rivaled what I saw on the screen before me.

I shook my head at the fact that they both had disappeared in a matter of two weeks. This was some wild shit going on here. The odds didn't look too good in favor of them coming back home alive. I hated to think about it but it was the truth. The cold-hearted truth.

There was knock on my door alerting my attention to someone on the other side. Again, I didn't get visitors so I cautiously rose from my seat and made my way to the front door.

I looked at my monitor. To say I was shocked at who was at my door was an understatement. I began to get nervous. I didn't want to open the door but my car was outside. They knew that I was home. Something told me that they weren't leaving until they spoke to me. I hesitantly opened the door.

"Hey, Troy." I smiled. "What can I do for you?" I didn't have the door open all of the way. I wanted him to get the impression that I was busy or that I didn't want to be disturbed.

"I need to come in for a minute and speak to you about something important. It's about Ashley's disappearance." He looked sincere so I stepped back, opened the door, and watched him walk past me and into my living room area.

"Is everything okay?" My heart started to thump in my chest. I didn't need to hear any bad news right now. Again, any stress could cause me to miscarry.

"Yes." He nodded his head. "It will be soon," he said as he walked in the direction of my television.

"I need to show you something important," he said as he pushed the power button to my Blu-ray disc player, opened the disc drawer, and placed a disc in the drawer and pushed the play button.

"Really." I looked at him funny because I was wondering why he was here and instead of at the Black family residence.

"Yes; where is your remote?" he asked as he took a seat on my sofa that was directly in front of the plasma television.

I handed him the remote and sat down on the same sofa with a cushion's length in between the both of us. My mind was all over the place as the video on the disc came on to the scene. There was no sound but I was familiar with what was playing on the screen. It made me tense up.

He fast-forwarded it to the part that made me hop up out of my seat.

"I think you better sit back down and start explaining to me what is really going on."

"I don't know what you are talking about." I spoke defiantly with my arms crossed against my chest. I was not going to be a snitch on myself. Wasn't even going to happen. He could forget about it.

"Sit the fuck down, now." He spoke with authority that made me do as I was instructed. "You have everybody fooled. Even me for such a long time. I would have never thought in a million years that you would be so capable of such things."

"I still don't know what you are talking about." I crossed one of my legs on top of the other and continued playing my ignorance very well.

"You are a cold-blooded killer, that is what you are. You have been killing all of these chicks to get at your obsession, Alex Black. It all came together in my mind when I looked at this footage that puts you at the scene of the crime and at the exact time of the crime. Your ass is going to jail for a very long time. We are going to pin all of this on you. You are a cold-hearted bitch." He looked at me with disdain.

I looked at him unmoved by the words that he was saying. He wasn't talking about me.

"Good thing is that no one knows it's you yet but me." He smiled. "I can use you on the last leg of my plans."

"Man, you have lost your mind if you think you pinning any of this on me. I'm not going out like that." I spoke confidently.

"I am glad that you think that but I know otherwise." He spoke as he reached in his pocket.

The next thing I knew he was lunging toward me with some type of cloth in his hand. He aimed right for my mouth with success. I tried to fight but it was futile. I faded into darkness instantly.

I was awakened by the smell of smelling salts under my nose. I instantly popped up and looked around the room in a frenzy. I didn't know how much time had passed but I knew something wasn't right as I became fully awake.

"You have a nice little shrine to Alex back there in your room I see. I think I got enough pictures in my phone to get you sent up the river for a very long time." He smiled smugly. "And these shoes are going to the lab to be tested for shoe prints you left on the body of the last victim. You were good but you weren't good enough." He laughed.

"You can't search my house or leave with any of my property without a warrant. It is against the law." I looked at him with a "fuck you" smile on my face. I had caught him. I knew my rights. I'd watched too much *Law & Order* to not know some of the basic laws.

"Too bad you didn't get all of the information, Jasmine, or you would know that under exigent circumstances or where the public safety may be in jeopardy I can do what I want and leave with what I may see as evidence. Read all of the law if you want to get by in this world."

I was speechless. I couldn't argue with him because I was stumped. He had won. "What can I do to make this go away?"

"Don't worry about that right now. Be ready to go into duty when I call you."

"How do I know that you won't turn me in when all of this is over?"

"You don't." He looked at me and laughed. "Isn't life grand? Some people fuck and the rest get fucked over. You, my dear, have just been fucked over."

He left me standing there as he walked toward the front door. I wasn't going down for this. I would go on the run first. I had some money saved up and it was enough to last me for a minute.

He turned before he opened the door to leave. "Don't even think about skipping town on me. That wouldn't be a good decision to make and I'm sure you want to be a free lady as long as possible. Rest easy."

I looked at the door as he left and closed it behind him. I was in complete shock and awe. What a tangled web we weave when first we practice to deceive.

Chapter 40

Troy

Moving Forward

I exited Jasmine's house all smiles two days ago. I wasn't expecting to find all of the things that I found that day. The evidence in that place was off of the hook. Her obsession for Alex rivaled my own obsession for revenge on the siblings. She was a walking time bomb that already had exploded. I was amazed at all of the crazy that was behind those beautiful eyes and face. You would never know she was that disturbed by the way she carried herself. I simply marveled.

I also went to check on the feisty Diana Black. She was holding up pretty well under the circumstances. Everything was setting up very nicely. I was actually giddy on the inside. Almost hated to see it all end. Almost.

I racked my brain relentlessly trying to figure out a way to find some information on Ashley's disappearance. Who could have been involved in this?

"Oh, shit. Maybe the chick I bumped into at that restaurant awhile back with Ashley might have something to do with her disappearance." I didn't know why that didn't come across my mind sooner. I was hopeful as I packed up a few of my things and took a trip back to the restaurant.

It took me about forty-five minutes to get to the restaurant because of traffic. I hated Baltimore traffic.

I got out of my car and made my way into the establishment. It was as I remembered it from before. It was moderately busy as I entered and waited to get the attention of the hostess at the front.

"Hello, sir, how can I help you today?" The pretty female greeted me with a smile.

"Hi, I'm Detective Lee. I need to speak to the owner or whoever is in charge at the moment."

"Sure, hold on for one second," she said and then turned her back to make a call on the phone that was located behind her. She said a few words that I didn't pay attention to because there was an attractive young male looking in my direction. He was with someone but he gazed at me for a few seconds and then his attention went back to the person he was here with.

"Sir?" I heard the young lady call out to me breaking me out of my trance. "My boss will be with you shortly. He asked if you could take a seat in the waiting area for a few minutes as he makes himself available."

"Sure." I nodded my head. "No problem at all."

A few minutes passed before a thin white man, maybe about in his late forties, walked up to me. "Detective Lee?"

"Yes." I stood up and reached out to shake his hand. "How are you today?"

"I'm doing well. Is there something that I can help you with?" he asked. He had a concerned look on his face. I was betting he was wondering if this was personal or business related. It was the way most people looked when they were approached by someone of law enforcement. It never changed and it didn't matter when it came to ethnicity either. The law made people uneasy.

"Yes, but I need to speak to you in a private setting," I insisted.

"Sure, follow me," he said as he turned and led the way through the restaurant, through the kitchen, and into a small office located in the back. "Please have a seat." He pointed to a chair in front of a small desk as he sat down behind it.

"I'm actually here to inquire of an employee of yours."

"Who might that be?" he asked.

"Well, there was a, I presume, black female chef who works here who I needed to get in contact with."

"You must be talking about Antoinette," he said, giving me her name. Information I didn't have.

"Is she the only female chef that you have on staff here?" I inquired.

"Yes, she was," he said disheartened.

"Was?" I asked.

"Yes, she gave me her leave notice about a week ago. She said that she needed a change in her life and that she was moving out of state to get a fresh start on life. She apologized for leaving me high and dry. I can't say I was happy with her decision because she was a great worker and person. She never gave me any problems. It is going to be tough to replace her. Why are you asking about her? Is she in some type of trouble?"

"I am not at liberty to say anything about that. Can you give me her last name?"

"Her name is Antoinette Andrews."

"I am grateful for your cooperation today. It was very helpful," I said as I got up out of my chair and reached over the desk to shake his hand.

"It was no problem at all. I hope that everything is okay with her," he said with a hopeful smile.

"I'm sure everything will be fine," I said with a smile to ease his mind. Too bad those were not the thoughts I was having in my mind. She was as good as dead in my book.

I exited the establishment, got into my car, and pulled off toward the precinct. Now that I had her name all I had to do was research her information and go looking for her. I was hoping that she hadn't skipped town like she had told her boss. I was screwed if that was the truth.

I was back at my office desk in about a half hour. Traffic was light because it was so close to noon. I logged on to my search database and keyed in her information and got all the information I needed within a matter of a half hour. I also received the surveillance video from the neighborhood where Ashley had gone missing. It had a good shot of the scene as Ashley was abducted. The person in the video chucked her phone in the water and then grabbed her and stuffed her in the rear of a vehicle. I amazed that no one saw this, but it was late at night in a predominately quiet neighborhood. The person got away without a hitch. I couldn't have done it better myself.

Everything was falling into place. I was back out of my office by two in the afternoon with a list of previous addresses in hand. This chick lived all over this city. I was up for the task.

I had been through some of the toughest parts of the city looking for Antoinette and Ashley or any sign of the vehicle. It was getting late and I was becoming more and more discouraged as time went on.

I had gotten several calls from members of the Black family asking me if there was any progress going on in the search with Ashley or Diana. I sorrowfully replied with the lack of any progress in either disappearance. I was sure this family was breaking apart at the seams with the things going on. Any family would be on edge waiting for any news of hope. I wasn't going to be delivering hope. I was going after my own justice and they would have to suffer as the justice I'd deliver became apparent in the end. The dead bodies and memories would be all that they had left.

It was getting late and the last house I was going to was in the suburbs. I drove down the street slowly as I approached the residence. This was a neighborhood of detached houses. Perfect for doing the unthinkable, namely kidnapping and killing. I drove past once and noticed a vehicle that looked similar to the one in the video surveillance footage.

I parked my vehicle a few cars down, got out of the car with my silencer-enhanced gun on my person, and casually walked back to the residence. I didn't know what was going to happen but I hoped that Ashley and this chick were still in here and Ashley was unharmed.

I walked up to the door with my gun in hand and knocked. There was silence for a few seconds. I knocked again but harder than before.

"Who is it?" The person who sounded like a woman answered the door.

"I'm looking for my son. He said this is where he was going to be with a friend of his," I lied.

"Don't no kids live here," she replied.

"Well, this is where he said he would be and I'm not leaving until I am sure he's not here. I'm about to call the police because I don't play when comes to my children," I threatened. There was a click or two and the door popped open enough for someone to pop their head out. I didn't hesitate once I knew that it was Antoinette. I quickly pulled my gun out and put my foot in the door preventing it from being closed.

"Back up and let me in or I will kill you," I threatened through clenched teeth. I didn't want to draw any attention in this direction.

She didn't hesitate as she pulled back and let me in. I closed the door. I didn't hesitate to aim the gun at her head and shoot before she could even get out another word, leaving her dead where she stood.

Chapter 41

Ashley

Rescued?

There was a knock on the door that both Antoinette and I heard. She put a finger up to her mouth signaling me to be quiet.

"Make any noise and I will not hesitate to end that noise with a bullet to the head," she threatened, as she retrieved her gun from the dresser drawer where she stored it and then placed it in the back of her pants. She left the room and made her way down the steps. I heard her say something but I didn't know what it was. I was hoping that it was someone here looking for me. There was another knock and then silence. I didn't hear anything else for a few seconds and I began to get nervous. I heard footsteps coming back up the stairs. The hope that I was feeling quickly dissipated. That was until I saw the face of Troy peek into the room with his gun in hand.

"Baby, I'm so glad to see you." I smiled and cried at the same time.

"I'm much gladder to see you," he said with a smile as bright as my own. "I didn't think I was going to find you," he said as he rubbed my face with the back of his hand ever so gently.

"I can't wait to see my family. Untie me, Troy, so we can get out of here. Where's Antoinette?" I asked. I didn't really care. I wanted to be sure she was no longer a threat.

"She's downstairs. She's no longer a threat."

"You knocked her out?"

"Permanently." He smiled. I didn't feel as happy as he did. I wanted her out of my life again, but not dead.

"Really?" I asked, shocked.

"I had to do it. She was in the way of my plans for you. For us," he said as he smiled. I couldn't help but feel special for someone to go to that length to get me back in their life.

"Well, you had to do what you had to do," I said as I pulled on the rope that Antoinette had me tied up to. "Baby, untie me so I can get dressed."

"Not yet," he said. "I have to do something first."

"What is that?" I said with an attitude.

"This." He raised the butt of the gun in the direction of my head. It didn't take me long to realize what was going to happen next. I had been here before.

I awoke tied up in a room and the muffled moans of another person caused me to focus my eyes. I had a splitting headache, but my heart fluttered with joy as I saw my slightly malnourished-looking sister Diana tied up in the same manner that I was. I was so glad that she was alive, but I was more curious as to why we both were tied up like we were. I know Troy was behind this but I didn't know why.

There is always someone looking for payback, always someone hunting for blood. Always! That was the only thought I could think right now. It was the only reason why we were here.

I heard footsteps once more, getting closer and closer to the room we were located in. The person entered the room. It was Troy. He had on a smug smile on his face. If the look in my eyes could have killed him he would have been dead.

"I guess you are wondering why you are here?" He laughed a little before he spoke again. It was a weird laugh. Like he was a lunatic or something. "Well right now is not the time to let you know the reason. I have one more piece to the puzzle to get together and then I will direct the final scene of your lives. I bet you didn't see this one coming."

I lunged toward him in the chair with all of my strength but I did get anywhere at all. He had us bound really well. I couldn't believe that I was freed from one captor only to be placed in captivity once more. This was the third time that I had been in a tied up chair situation and as the saying goes, three strikes and you're out.

This was kidnapping situation number three for me. The first two escapes/rescues were good. But I need a sure enough miracle right now. We both did. So I closed my eyes and began to pray like never before. I didn't know how long I was praying but I did it loudly and I guessed it pushed Troy out of the room or house for all that matters, because when I finished and opened my eyes he was no longer in the room. I looked at Diana who was crying and it looked like she had been crying the whole time she was in here because her eye sockets were very swollen. I could only imagine the thoughts and feeling she went through all of this time here all by herself. It had to be pure hell. Damn near insanity.

It grew dark in the room and the realization that Troy had left us alone brought no consolation to me. No one knew we were out here. We were left to see how this was going to play out. Fear set in as the minutes ticked past. Dread and wonder of what was to come invaded my every thought.

Chapter 42

Alex

Clueless

A day or two went past and once again I was sitting in my parents' living room waiting for a word from somebody, anybody, on my sisters' disappearances.

Presently, I had two sisters missing, a mother very close to losing her sanity, a father who was too quiet, and a younger brother and sister looking to me for answers. Wallace was deep in thought as well. He was sitting in the corner of the room with his hand on his chin and his eyes closed. Troy had stopped through yesterday with no good news and Jasmine was missing in action.

"I'm going to step outside for a moment," I said to no one in particular. Everyone's eyes shot toward me. I focused on the look of my mother's eyes the most. It was filled with tears.

"Mom, I'm going to step right outside the door for a breath of fresh air," I said as I walked over to reassure her. I kneeled down, cupped her hands into mine, and kissed her on the forehead. "I won't go any farther." She pulled me in for a tight hug and I looked at my father before I walked out of the room.

If I were a cigarette smoker, right now would have been the time that I would have inhaled a few of them back to back. The tension was so thick in the room. The police were no help to us right now. They were as clueless as we were. There weren't a lot of clues to go on anyway. Troy had been out on the prowl looking for Ashley with no hope.

I wasn't standing outside but a few minutes before Wallace came outside to join me. "How are you holding up?" he said as he stood next to me a few seconds before he started to talk.

"Man, this is some wild mess here." I shook my head. "Wilder than California."

"I don't know about that, but this situation is running neck and neck in the 'what in the hell is going on' category." He let out a slight chuckle. He was trying to lighten the mood I guessed. It was a nice try since the statement was true.

"Yes, that is true." I wanted to smile, but it wasn't happening. "We had a crazy time in Cali early on. Drama." I huffed. "It seemed like all we come up against is drama. We go to school in another state and drama is there. We move back home and now some more drama has popped off here. What is it with this family and drama?" I rambled on.

"Every family has drama. It's a part of life." Wallace shook his head. "You know I know all about it."

"Yes, but damn, man. Can't we get a break? This is some heavy things going on. I feel like death is looming around and is getting ready to rear its ugly head." My voice trembled. The thought terrified me. "I'm not built for all of this. Nobody is. Somebody has it out for this family and I don't know why. This is not random. And the reasons could be anything," I said as I looked at him in fear and panic.

"That's why if you have to go anywhere you don't go alone and never deviate without letting someone know. We have to keep everyone close and keep an eye out for anything. Whoever's involved will slip up eventually. We have to be focused." He always sounded so grounded and confident. It was definitely needed right now.

"Wallace, all of what you are saying is true. I don't know if I'm coming or going right now. I don't know who's who and what's what. I'm clueless. I'm the nosey one and I'm clueless. That is not a good look right now."

"Nobody has it all any of the time. Only God. You are not alone in this. Even though it is tough right now your family is tough as nails and you all will make it through this. I know you will," he said as he patted me on my shoulder. I felt a slight relief. I was wondering how long it would last.

"You are right. We have some tough blood running through our veins. We are survivors." I nodded my head in confidence.

"Alex, I really have to say that I am proud of the way you are holding things down right now. I have seen stronger men fall under lighter pressures." We looked at each other as he spoke. I could feel the authenticity of his words. Again, they lifted my spirits a bit.

"Thanks, I can't take the credit. God got me." I smiled. "We will survive this." I smiled even harder. But my mind was saying, *I hope so.*

"You will. I can feel it."

"Great." I turned to go back in the house. "Let's get back in here and look for some more clues on Ashley's laptop and get something to eat. I am starving."

"Cool. I'll order some pizza for the whole house," Wallace said as he walked into the house with me.

Chapter 43

Jasmine

Gone Fishing

I was sitting in my bedroom with the lights off. It was completely dark in my room. I was deep in thought. All of my plans fell through with the exception of the one growing in my body. I sobbed uncontrollably at the fact that my fate was in the hands of another man. One whose was more incoherent than my own. I didn't know what Troy had cooked up but I was now an instrument in his plans. I was going down one way or the other. I didn't plan for this.

Out of nowhere I began to hear the maniacal laughter of my mother's voice all over the room.

"Stop it! Stop it! Stop it!" I moaned as I covered my ears and rocked back and forth. It felt like my mind was unhinging.

I had been in this room, stark naked, for close to two days, my mind going round and round in thought, my past mixing with the present. I was on edge. I had my cell phone taped to my breast so that I wouldn't misplace it.

Waiting on this phone call was chauffeuring me around in the mazes of my mind. I tried my best not to think about instability of my mind. My plans for Alex and me had kept me focused for so long that I didn't really have to worry about it, but now I was staring it in the face. I was the crazy girl I tried to hide so well. I was the one who needed to be medicated. My mother was right. I was her. I was going to end up the same way that she was right now.

I wasn't going to bring a child into this mess to suffer the way that I had for so long. I changed my mind. I didn't want this to happen. I was going to end it for both of us. Right now.

"I'm sorry, baby Lexington." I rubbed my stomach. "I thought this is what I wanted, but I was wrong."

I rose up from the bed, out of my bedroom, and walked into my kitchen area. Tears flowed from my eyes as I reached into one of my drawers for a butcher's knife. "I'm not fit to be your mother or to be alive," I whispered. I palmed the knife firmly in my hands and raised it above my head to get a good momentum for the fatal blow.

I was startled by vibration of the phone taped to my breast, causing me to jump and drop the knife. I snatched the phone off of my body. I should have been in pain but I was numb to it all at the moment. The pain of my choices had hit me hard. I was remorseful for all of the lives that I took to make me comfortable. The lives I took to get a man who didn't want me. I was a living, breathing fool.

"Hello," I answered the phone. The enthusiasm of life I had days before had all but left my voice.

"You ready?" Troy asked.

"Yes."

"Well hop in your car and meet me at the address I'm going to text you in a few seconds. You have fifteen minutes." He hung up in my ear.

I looked at the phone, wondering once again how the tables got turned so quickly. But I knew all too well that you reap what you sow. I was now reaping all of it at once. At least that was what it felt like.

I dressed quickly without even washing up or combing my hair. I was a mess. I hopped into my car in just jeans and a pink T-shirt. I looked at myself in the mirror and didn't recognize the girl I saw. The one I now saw looked broken and defeated.

"I'm sorry, Lexington, for almost ending your beautiful life before it even began. I am going to do one thing right in this world if it is the last thing I do. I'm going to bring in this world a healthy baby and give it to someone who would truly be a blessing to him or her," I said and then I let out a small smile. I reached into the glove compartment of my car and found a brush. I brushed my hair back as best I could and then pulled off toward my destination.

It was too late for me but it wasn't for my unborn child.

I pulled up to the predetermined destination and waited for what was next. A tap on the passenger side window caused me to jump. It was Troy.

"So glad you could make it," he said and then smirked.

"Yeah." I spoke nonchalantly.

"So let's get down to business. I need you to get Alex to meet you somewhere, alone, and then I need you to bring him to this address." He handed me a small piece of paper. I read the address quietly and remained that way until he spoke again.

"I will need you there within the next hour. Time is of the essence. Don't forget, if you try to run it will only anger me and then I will be forced to turn you in and that baby of yours will be an orphan. I know that's not what you want."

I silently shook my head from side to side, with hesitancy written all over my face. He didn't need to know my plans were the same.

"Oh, take this so that there will not be any reluctance on his part. You will have to use this, so don't be afraid to do so." He handed me a small Taser gun. "As soon as you help me you'll be a free woman and all of the evidence that I have against you will magically disappear. One hand washes the other."

I smiled and nodded my head. "Got it." I just wanted him to get out of the car. The Troy I knew before this was all but a memory. The Troy I was looking at now was more obsessed than I ever was. The look in his eyes was very shifty and almost empty of feeling.

He finally got out of the car. I sighed in relief and I pulled off in the direction of the Black residence. I didn't know how I was going to get Alex out of the house alone. This guy Wallace was with him everywhere he went since he'd gotten here. This was going to be a task.

I parked my car in front of the house. I had never been this nervous going into the Black residence. Maybe because most of the time I was entering the house with good intentions. This visit would be quite the opposite. I rang the doorbell and Li'l Shawn opened the door and peeked out. I could tell that Mrs. Black had everyone on lockdown and high alert. She had every right to do as she saw fit.

"Hey, Jasmine," he said and then pulled the door back to let me in. I rubbed my fingers in the palms of my hands a few times as I entered. I walked into the living room and there was only Alex and Brittany sitting in the room. Alex had the laptop in his lap while he was doing something with his phone. I was sure he was still in track down mode.

"Hey, everyone," I said trying to give off calmness. I sat down on the loveseat that was diagonally facing everyone. I was racking my brain with a way to get Alex out of this house without alarming anyone. "Hey, Alex. Where is Wallace?" I asked.

"Oh, he had to go take care of something. He'll be back shortly."

"Oh, okay." I pretended like I was watching television with Li'l Shawn and Brittany.

"Alex, I need a really huge favor. I know right now is not the time, but I need to go to the auto parts store for some new windshield wipers and I don't want to go in there alone. They try to take advantage of us females when we enter a store like that. I just want a guy with me so I don't get ripped off or leave with the wrong thing." I tried to put on a pitiful face.

"Your baby's father not available?" he asked me. It kind of took my breath away that he would ask me that.

"We're not on speaking terms at the moment," I answered.

"Well, take Li'l Shawn. He good with that stuff." It was like he was purposely trying to push me off on someone else. Next he would probably tell me take his little sister, Brittany.

"No offense to Li'l Shawn"—I looked in Li'l Shawn's direction—"but I really would appreciate it if you would go with me. I'm more comfortable with someone my age. But I understand if you don't have time for that at this moment." I tried to sound convincing. Truth was I was only six years older than they were.

I sat back in the seat I was in and focused on the television. I had a disappointed look on my face. I remained completely quiet. Men hated it when women got quiet on them but that didn't work on him for some reason. I guessed he really didn't want to do it. I guessed I had to pull out my last hope card.

"Alex, I just need this one favor from you. I think you owe me at least this one little thing since I helped you out . . . a few times I might add."

He looked at me for a few seconds. I thought he was in disbelief that I would bring up the favor he owed me at a time like this. I was desperate and desperate times called for desperate measures.

"Let's go," he said as he hopped up off of the chair. "We have to make this quick." He speed-walked toward the car.

I was all smiles on the inside. I couldn't believe that I got him out of the house. I hopped in the car and pulled off toward the destination I had already pressed into my GPS. I had the readout playing in my Bluetooth so that he wouldn't be cognizant of where I was headed until it was too late. I had the Taser in my side jacket pocket ready to zap him at the right time.

I drove for a few minutes and drove right past an auto parts shop.

"Jasmine, we just passed a shop," he said with a little irritation in his voice.

"I don't like that shop. A friend of mine told me to go to a particular shop."

"Why couldn't this friend go with you?"

I looked at him like he had lost his mind. "Because that friend is a woman and not a man." I gave back just as much attitude he gave me.

"I'm sorry, Jasmine," he apologized. "I'm just on edge right now."

"I know; I am as well. I'm trying to keep my mind on other things. And not the disappearance of my best friend. I thought that this small outing would get your mind off of things for at least a few seconds."

"I appreciate the thought."

"Alex, could you look under the seat and see if you see my ring underneath it?"

"Sure," he said as he bent over and reached under the seat for a ring that I didn't lose. I quickly pulled out the Taser, flipped in on with my thumb, and pressed it to his side. Several quick jolts was all that it took to knock him out. Mind you I was driving and doing this at the same time. I pushed him back in the seat so he wouldn't get any cramps or anything in the slumped-over position. I also didn't want to bring any attention toward us, namely the police.

It took about thirty-five minutes to get to this location where Troy gave me directions to. He had me driving up winding roads and whatnot to get to Upper Marlboro, Maryland. It was a highly rural area. Large houses on large plots of land with fields as far as the eye could see. I never even knew about this part of Maryland and it wasn't even that far away from Baltimore.

It was near dark when I pulled up. I spotted a car I assumed to be Troy's. I called his phone and let him know that I was outside with his precious cargo.

It didn't take him long to come out and hoist Alex over his shoulder and carry him into this old hillbilly-type home. It looked like it needed to be demolished or in need of a serious rehabilitation.

I stayed in the car hoping that he was finished with me, but he signaled me to come with him with the gun in his hand. I immediately followed suit. We walked into a mildew-smelling house that was still furnished with almost ancient-looking furniture partially covered with sheets. Up the stairs we went until we made it to a room with two individuals I knew very well. Ashley and Diana were tied up in chairs on the opposite sides of the room. There was a dresser with a vanity station and a mattress that looked to be covered with a dark stain in the middle of it. I cringed because it looked to be old blood. I knew the look of blood on a mattress and this was definitely it. It made me curious as to what happened to it. I had a feeling I was about to find out very soon.

Chapter 44

Troy

The Set

She's dead! That was what I thought as I sat inside of my car. Ma Dear had taken her last breath with me sitting beside her. She tried to hold on but the illness got the best of her. The nurses tried to console me but I was beyond it. I was disappointed that she didn't get to see this thing to the end. She wanted revenge so bad, but I guessed it was all on me now. Good thing everything was in place. I was doing part of this for her but it was mostly for me. I had my own agenda for payback that she didn't know about.

I sat in my car a few more minutes before I made my way to "the set" as I called it. As soon as I left Jasmine in the parking lot I made my way here to let her know that I was on my way to finish the plan that was set. I didn't know that I was actually going to see her taking her last breath. I actually wanted her to see the scene I had set up via video and then pass away. But, alas, it didn't work out so here I was going to finish it off myself.

I drove with a content beat flowing through my fingers, tapping on the steering wheel as I drove to my destination. I pulled up to my childhood home and looked at the building that was still standing but barely. We had moved out of it after the incident, but never sold it. All of my siblings moved far away and I was the only one who was looking after it now. I opened the still-creaky door and walked up the wooden steps to the room where it all happened. Where my life was changed. Where my destiny was taken away from me.

"Good evening, ladies," I greeted Ashley and Diana as I entered the room. They were nonresponsive because they were gagged. "I know you are wondering why you are here, but I can't tell you that until the final participants in this reenactment show up. I'm so glad that you could make the cut of this scene." I laughed heartily at my own joke. They didn't get it but they soon would. They all would actually.

I set up the camera that I had brought with me and rearranged the scene the way it was that night. I wanted it as I remembered it. There were going to be a few "extras" in the scene but they would serve their purpose. I got the call that I was waiting for and made my exit at stage right, down the stairs and out to the car to retrieve the last cast member. He was out of it but as soon as he woke he would wish he was still unconscious. He had the best part of the scene I was about to shoot. I hauled him up the wooden steps and into the room with the others. I tossed him on the bed and then tied his arms and his legs to the bed. I pulled down his pants and exposed his body from the waist down. The size of his manhood not aroused was quite impressive and perfect for the scene as well.

The extra, Jasmine, was standing in the doorway with a confused look on her face. She didn't know that her part in this scene was just widened a few seconds ago.

It didn't take long before Alex awakened from his slumber. He wasn't enthusiastic about his present state of being. "What the fuck is going on here?" he asked as he twisted to get himself free. He wasn't going anywhere because I had him tied up good.

I pulled the tape from Ashley's mouth and then Diana's. They all began to throw obscenities my way but the gun I pulled from behind me shushed them all.

"First let's start with the first question: who am I? Because I know you want to know who the hell I am. My name is Troy McNeal. Lee is my mother's maiden name."

"I don't give a shit who you are. Why the hell are we here?" Ashley spewed anger-filled words my way. The feeling was mutual.

"Why are you here?" I walked around the room a bit before I answered. I wanted to keep them in suspense for a while. "I am here for vengeance. I am here for blood. I am here because your father, James Parks, took something from me. But before I finish with the why let me give you some back story. A good movie is always good with some back story or a flashback scene. I love those in movies." I grinned as I thought back.

"My father was a really sick and perverted person. He was a pedophile of his children. The boys and the girls. He broke us all in sexually at the coming of age. He said he was doing us a favor. After he broke you in, he would treat you like royalty. You got whatever you wanted or asked for. Every child was given this opportunity. Every child would watch the end results of the other siblings' 'breaking in' and then watch them get all that their heart desired.

"My mother was treated less than equal in these situations, which she tolerated but secretly became jealous of us all. She was not an attractive person but she had money. Her family did. That's why my father married her. He wasn't a loafer; he had a job. A very good one. But none of this was enough for him; he had to go outside the lines and draw other people into the equation. That is where your father comes into the picture.

"That greedy bastard wanted too much and my father did what he had to do to cut him off. But that didn't stop your father from seeking vengeance. He crept in here one lowly night and took my inheritance from me. He took everything. I had to earn my own. I had to work my way up this pissy ladder of success to get to you all. But I made it and now I am going to end it all for you like your father ended mine the night he came in here and severed my inheritance.

"My father's name was Charles McNeal. He was a Bank of America employee. It was where he met your piece of scum of a father. I don't know what went wrong between them two but he came in here and cut off his dick with a knife, cutting off my chances at easy street and giving me the hardships of life. He was supposed to break me in. I was the last one. I watched from the shadows as he took revenge on my father. I was a quiet child and lurked around in the darkness with ease and agility. You see that night was the night it was supposed to happen. It was the day after my twelfth birthday and he promised to come in and give me my inheritance. But James Parks came in and cut it off. He cut it off!"

I was quiet for a few seconds as I stared at them all one by one. They looked horrified at my tale, but it was my family and my legacy. I was cheated and now they must die for it since their father was gone. They were next in line.

"So we are in here because our biological father cut some man's dick off in revenge?" Ashley asked me. She looked at me as if I was crazy. "You have got to be fucking kidding me. All of this because your sick-ass father didn't get to fuck you. You are a lunatic. Who does this type of shit? This is what I get for dating a white guy. I wanted to be different, give it a try. I knew you was too good to be true, but I went against my better judgment and all I have been through and threw caution to the wind and here I am now: tied the fuck up once again."

The youngest of the siblings was sobbing in the corner that she was in.

"Don't worry, baby Diana. It will all be over soon. I'm going to be getting rid of some bad blood out of this world very soon. James Park's bad blood will be cut off when I end your lives. I am going to start with Alex and his manhood. Jasmine is going to do me a favor and get that monster to its full size and then it's off with its head and you will watch him bleed to death." I laughed out loud. Alex didn't look too thrilled though.

"Next, I'm going to stuff the severed flesh in your mouth like I found my mother that night, Ashley. And then shoot you in the head. Finally the youngest gets the easy way out. Just a bullet to the head. That works for me. And to wrap the scene up, the wonderful Jasmine will be taking the rap for all of this because she is the master mind behind all of the killings you see, Alex."

He looked at me and then at her in shock. "Yes, Alex, this girl is in love with you. Infatuated even. She was killing up more chicks than Jeffrey Dahmer did them gay boys back in the seventies, eighties, and nineties. Sorry, Jasmine, I lied. You going down for a long time. I, on the other hand, walked into all of this mess on a hunch and caught you after the act. What a sad way to end up. But I don't give a shit. I will be free of the nightmares and you all will be dead and in jail. Case closed.

"So go on over there, Jasmine, and get this scene rolling so I can get on with my life." I motioned with the gun. She hesitantly did as instructed. I knew she was enjoying it on the inside though. She worked feverishly as his manhood began to expand. I looked on in awe at the size. The two sisters had their eyes tightly closed. I guessed they didn't want to see their brother getting a blow job.

"All right, Jasmine, that's enough." She got up and wiped the saliva away from the sides of her mouth. "Now it's time for you to feel the pain that my father felt that night and scream like he did as well. Too bad no one heard him but us. And that will be the same thing that happens tonight."

"No, the fuck it won't. You won't be doing any of that." Wallace appeared out of nowhere. "This is the end of the road for you."

"Yes, you are going down for a very long time." Nelson walked through the door to the room. Both of them had guns in their hands. "So get your shitty hands in the air. You are under arrest.

"We had you under investigation the whole time. You thought you were fucking me over, but I in turn was doing it to you. A friend of my father, Wallace, was in town and came to see me down at the precinct. He said he had some bad vibes about you. I was doing my own research as well. I started running and digging into your logins at work with the permission of the chief, who didn't like you to start with, and found out that you were doing a lot of monitoring of the Black family's whereabouts. We got a warrant to raid your house this morning and found all types of good stuff to put you away for a very long time. You probably will never see the light of day with all the things going on with you. Man, you are one sick prick. Too bad though because the wood you had was good. What a waste." He laughed.

I was handcuffed and put in the back of the police car right beside Jasmine. She sobbed all the way down to the lockup. I on the other hand was not going to show any emotion. I was going to take it like a man as I had done up to now.

Jasmine's Epilogue

They say confession is good for the soul. I was now sitting on death row waiting for my turn to be put to death. I confessed to multiple counts of premeditated murder. I know what you are saying. Why didn't I take the insanity plea? It was simple. That would have made me like my mother. Weak. Insanity was for the weak and I was not going out like that. That was my logic. I had to make it known that I did all I did for the man I wanted. Was I crazy? Delusional? Or just a ride or die chick? The choice is yours to believe what you want to believe. I say I am a ride or die chick.

I would have done anything to get Alex. That was why I when I gave birth to twin baby boys, I signed them over to him. I wrote him and broke down the details of my impregnation and asked him for his forgiveness. I received a letter from him with that forgiveness.

Ironically, I received another letter from my mother letting me know that she was released a few weeks ago for my father's murder. She had done her time in the mental institution and now was free. I, on the other hand, was now waiting for my life to end.

I was now sitting in a waiting room for her to come and see me. I was only allowed one visitor a month. Ashley came and saw me a few months ago and now it was her turn.

I watched the door as it opened. I was in a single-door room with a thick piece of glass that stood between us.

She walked over with an emotionless face. I was already seated and waiting for this moment to be over. I only allowed this meeting to get the air between us cleared. She said she had something to say to me. I was curious as to what it was.

"Hello, baby," she greeted me. She had pity in her eyes. I hated pity. "How are you holding up?"

I rolled my eyes and then answered, "Don't pretend to care. Say what you have to say so I can leave this earth in peace."

"Don't talk like that. I love you, Jasmine. You are my only child. My shining star. I can't believe things ended up for you like this. This wasn't the plan I had for your life. I wanted more for you. Do you feel sorry for the things that you have done?"

I looked at her for a few moments, because I really didn't have much remorse for my action. I did it with purpose. "Sometimes," I mumbled. It was a true statement that I struggled with most of the days in this place.

"Baby, you ask God for forgiveness? He will forgive you. He forgave me." She looked sincere as she spoke.

"Forgiveness can't bring my father back can it?"

"Jasmine, I take the blame for my actions. I told you that I was sorry for that. What more do you want?"

"I want your soul to burn in hell. And then burn some more." I got up from my seat and walked away from her. My eyes watered with tears. The hate and pain I carried would be buried with me.

Troy's Epilogue

I would be spending my whole natural life in prison for kidnapping, criminal conspiracy, and murder. I had a lot of time to reflect behind these iron bars. Most of all, I thought about if all of this was worth my freedom. To be spoiled and broken in by my father was immoral and unfathomable by the world's standards. A family with those types of problems was instantly shunned in the world. They said that I was mentally unstable and would need years and years of counseling to even touch the surface of my problems and mode of thinking.

They played back the audio of the speech that I recorded on the night of my capture in that room with the Black family siblings. The looks on the faces of the jury were ones of pure horror and pity. I held my head high as I was the only one in my family to even be in the room for the trial. None of my siblings called or showed their faces. I didn't expect them to do either. But I did get one letter from one of them. It was a letter that was filled with regret and remorse.

My oldest sibling, the one who wrote the letter, explained to me in great detail why he went away all those years ago, never to return. He wrote of years and years of mental reconstruction therapy along with tons of medication that was only a mild answer to his sleepless nights and rampant promiscuity. He spoke of his terror as he watched his brothers and sister be treated the way that he was and act as if they were all the better for it. He went on to tell me of how all of them were in the same boat and he was happy that my father didn't get a chance to do the same things to me. But said that he looked up my case particulars online and read about my pursuant behavior for my so-called inheritance. He was glad that I was caught and that I would have a better chance at a sane life than he would ever hope to have.

I read the letter several times and felt the hurt and pain that was poured onto the pages with eloquent words. It made me think but I was still curious of the inheritance aspect of it all. Yes, I would need a great deal of counseling and purging to get to a clean state of mind. Here I was thinking that I was ridding the world of the so-called bad blood in James Parks's offspring when I should have been concerned with my own bloodline.

Alex's Epilogue

Fragile.

That was the one word that described me right now. I still couldn't believe it. I had not one but two mouths to feed. The news of their presence on this earth brought me to my knees, literally. I couldn't believe that I was a father. I was reckless and wild. But those days were now behind me and it was involuntarily. If this was God's way of getting my attention, then He had it.

When Jasmine wrote me the letter informing me of the paternity on my end, there were some doubts there. It was enough to take a few days off and get some time to myself. How could a person take that type of information and not respond with some uncertainty? I knew that as soon as the babies arrived and the looks on their faces made me melt instantly they made me weak with emotion. I cried like the babies that they were for days and the blessing that they were. I took a paternity test and they came back a 99 percent positive match for me being the father. Lexington and Lacey were their names and they were definitely my weakness.

I sat in the living room of my parents' house as each of my family members took turns holding and spoiling them to death. My parents were just as shocked as I was when it came to the news.

"Look at them, they are just so precious. Shawn, can you believe we are grandparents?" my mother said with a proud smile on her face as she looked at my father.

"No. I still can't believe it." He smiled too. "Though I was sure that it was going to be Ashley who started us off down the road that leads to rocking chairs and Depends." Everyone in the room laughed at my father's remarks. It was a joyous time for us all at the moment. Babies always brought joy, even into the most grievous situations. And considering that three of their children almost lost their lives a little less than nine months ago, this was a very momentous time in all of our lives.

We were still a family. The Black family. Ups and downs, kidnappings, adultery, fornication, homosexuality, murder, and betrayal; we survived them all. God was definitely on our side. We didn't know what tomorrow would hold but we knew that we had each other through it all.

I looked across the room at my twin, my ace, my other half. She was one of my favorite people. Not because she was a family member but because she wasn't letting any of the past hold her back from living. She was back to work and even considering dating again. Troy really had us fooled. Who would have known all of that was going on behind the closed doors of his family's home? We all had problems within our family, some more tumultuous than others, but nothing was insurmountable in my eyes. A family who stuck together could make it through anything.

Ashley's Epilogue

I looked around the room at all of the family in the room. There were now four generations in the room. I was in awe that I was still alive to tell you the truth. Troy had us all fooled, even himself. When you think that you are the smartest and untouchable is when you become your weakest. He underestimated the power of family and how tough we were. Death had come my way too many times for me not to be conscious of who I dated from now on. Oh, yes, I was going to start dating again, but a lot slower and with little expectation. I tried to move past my demons so fast that I set myself up for anything. Not that I could control any of it. It's just that not taking your time and being honest with oneself could lead to situations just like this one or worse.

I was now an auntie and I was loving every minute of it. My brother was going to be a great father, but I knew that it would be a challenge for him to slow down his fast-paced lifestyle. He said that it would be no problem to do so now but I would definitely have a talk with him about it all. This new situation would make us closer for sure. He would need all of the help he could get.

My mind wandered on to Jasmine and all that was revealed about her and her obsession for my brother. I was quite shocked to know how deep the obsession went. I went to see her a few months back and to see her behind bars awaiting death was bone chilling. That could have easily been me, if I continued down the path that I was on a few years ago. It was only by God's grace that I was not in that type of situation now. I surely knew that I deserved it. Maybe all of this was a lesson for me to pull back and let God continue to lead my life. I thought that was it. I had made a mess of it so far; now I had to be patient and wait for Him. A big smile covered my face at the thought of inner peace and no pressure when it came to a mate. There was one out there and I was sure he would be the right one for me.

"Hand me Lexington." I reached out to my mother who was showering him with kisses. She handed him to me and then almost snatched Lacey from my father. We all laughed at the look on his face.

"I see I am going have to fight you for my grandbabies now." He laughed.

"Don't start nothing and it won't be nothing." She laughed and everyone else followed suit afterward.

"I trump all of you," my grandmother boasted. "Hand me both of them babies before I turn this mother out." We all laughed as the babies were instantly passed her way.

This was my family. We were blood through it all. Nothing could tear us apart. We were here to stay. Four generations strong.

ORDER FORM
URBAN BOOKS, LLC
97 N18th Street
Wyandanch, NY 11798

Name (please print):_____

Address: _____

City/State: _____

Zip: _____

QTY	TITLES	PRICE
	16 On The Block	$14.95
	A Girl From Flint	$14.95
	A Pimp's Life	$14.95
	Baltimore Chronicles	$14.95
	Baltimore Chronicles 2	$14.95
	Betrayal	$14.95
	Bi-Curious	$14.95
	Bi-Curious 2: Life After Sadie	$14.95
	Bi-Curious 3: Trapped	$14.95
	Both Sides Of The Fence	$14.95
	Both Sides Of The Fence 2	$14.95
	California Connection	$14.95

Shipping and handling: add $3.50 for 1st book, then $1.75 for each additional book.

Please send a check payable to:

Urban Books, LLC

Please allow 4-6 weeks for delivery

ORDER FORM
URBAN BOOKS, LLC
97 N18th Street
Wyandanch, NY 11798

Name (please print):_____

Address: _____

City/State: _____

Zip: _____

QTY	TITLES	PRICE
	California Connection 2	$14.95
	Cheesecake And Teardrops	$14.95
	Congratulations	$14.95
	Crazy In Love	$14.95
	Cyber Case	$14.95
	Denim Diaries	$14.95
	Diary Of A Mad First Lady	$14.95
	Diary Of A Stalker	$14.95
	Diary Of A Street Diva	$14.95
	Diary Of A Young Girl	$14.95
	Dirty Money	$14.95
	Dirty To The Grave	$14.95

Shipping and handling: add $3.50 for 1st book, then $1.75 for each additional book.

Please send a check payable to:

Urban Books, LLC

Please allow 4-6 weeks for delivery

ORDER FORM
URBAN BOOKS, LLC
97 N18th Street
Wyandanch, NY 11798

Name (please print):_____

Address: _____

City/State: _____

Zip: _____

QTY	TITLES	PRICE
	Gunz And Roses	$14.95
	Happily Ever Now	$14.95
	Hell Has No Fury	$14.95
	Hush	$14.95
	If It Isn't love	$14.95
	Kiss Kiss Bang Bang	$14.95
	Last Breath	$14.95
	Little Black Girl Lost	$14.95
	Little Black Girl Lost 2	$14.95
	Little Black Girl Lost 3	$14.95
	Little Black Girl Lost 4	$14.95
	Little Black Girl Lost 5	$14.95

Shipping and handling: add $3.50 for 1st book, then $1.75 for each additional book.
Please send a check payable to:
   Urban Books, LLC
Please allow 4-6 weeks for delivery

ORDER FORM
URBAN BOOKS, LLC
97 N18th Street
Wyandanch, NY 11798

Name (please print):_____

Address: _____

City/State: _____

Zip: _____

QTY	TITLES	PRICE
	Loving Dasia	$14.95
	Material Girl	$14.95
	Moth To A Flame	$14.95
	Mr. High Maintenance	$14.95
	My Little Secret	$14.95
	Naughty	$14.95
	Naughty 2	$14.95
	Naughty 3	$14.95
	Queen Bee	$14.95
	Say It Ain't So	$14.95
	Snapped	$14.95
	Snow White	$14.95

Shipping and handling: add $3.50 for 1st book, then $1.75 for each additional book.
Please send a check payable to:
    Urban Books, LLC
Please allow 4-6 weeks for delivery